WOLF RANCH: RAVENOUS

WOLF RANCH
BOOK 9

RENEE ROSE

VANESSA VALE

WANT FREE RENEE ROSE BOOKS?

Receive a slew of free Renee Rose books: Go to http://sub scribepage.com/alphastemp to sign up for Renee Rose's newsletter and receive free books. In addition to the free stories and bonus material, you will also get special pricing, exclusive previews and news of new releases.

Did you know you can buy direct from Renee Rose? Get signed books, special editions, and heavily discounted bundles. Use this coupon for an additional 10% discount on your entire order - **READER10** or go here https://shop. reneeroseromance.com/discount/READER10

1

WES

I TURNED off the water and slid the shower curtain back. Steam had fogged up the small bathroom and coated the mirror. I stepped out onto the bathmat, grabbed a towel– one of Remy's pink ones–and started to dry off.

Moving sucked. Moving as a single parent with a four-year-old was even harder.

I'd found the sheets, the pots and pans, the toiletries. All important things. But the box full of stuffed animals was missing or at least hadn't been unearthed from the pile still filling the living room.

It had been a crisis, the missing box. Still was.

I'd gotten Remy to sit in her booster that lifted her up to the right height at the kitchen table and color while I showered the sweat and dirt from hauling boxes and rearranging furniture.

As a shifter, lifting heavy things was easy, but in July, it still brought out some sweat.

I swiped the mirror with my towel, then rubbed at my hair.

As I stared at my half-fogged reflection, I couldn't miss how fucking tired I looked. I was a father, not a grandpa.

I took the day off to move, but Remy still needed dinner. Her own bath. Finding that missing stuffed animal box. Plus, I had to be up at Wolf Ranch at dawn. My responsibilities, here at home and at the ranch as the foreman, never ended.

"Food," I grumbled to myself. "You need food, a beer, and some TV that doesn't involve cartoons or princesses." I wrapped my towel around my waist. Barely. I glanced down. I was not made for a pink toddler towel.

"Remy, what do you say to hamburgers for dinner?" I called.

She didn't answer, which was a surprise because even though she was a tiny thing, she loved to eat. And being a shifter pup, she loved meat. She also loved to talk. To me. To herself. To her stuffed animals.

"Remy?" I came down the hall from the bedrooms, hand on the towel at my hip.

The one-story rancher I bought was in town on a nice lot. I'd chosen it because it had been completely renovated–new everything–which meant I didn't have to spend any time fixing leaky faucets or updating an outdated bathroom. The location was perfect to get Remy to school, hang out with friends when she was older, and do all the kid things living isolated on a ranch didn't offer. I'd waited to buy a house and move our shit out of storage until I was sure it was going to work out with the new job and pack.

It seemed we'd struck gold with the Wolf Ranch pack. They'd welcomed us both like we were family, not perfect strangers, who also happened to be shifters.

The routine and closeness was just the change Remy and I needed after being on the rodeo circuit for six months out of the year. Plus, things had gotten weird in our home pack. I'd heard that Remy's mom had shown back up, and I hadn't wanted her messing with our daughter's head. Hell, I didn't even want Remy to meet her.

It was hard enough that I had to explain to my daughter why her mom wasn't around. The last thing our pup needed was to feel that abandonment more acutely after meeting her mom and having her skip town again. It was one thing to be abandoned when she was three weeks old. A four-year-old remembered everything. And everyone.

"Remy?"

When she didn't answer again, I picked up my pace and frowned. The kitchen was empty. Her coloring was on the table, crayons strewn over the wood surface.

"Remy!" I called again.

She was probably playing hide and seek with me. Or was just absorbed in whatever imaginative play she had going on at the moment. Maybe she'd fallen asleep after exhausting herself with that meltdown over the stuffed animals.

But as I made a quick scan of each room and didn't find her, the hair on the back of my neck started to rise.

Fuck.

She wouldn't have left the house. With all the changes

lately, she'd been more clingy. She hadn't wanted to leave my side. Hell, she'd been whiny about me leaving her to get into the shower.

Now, my heart rate surged. My inner wolf grew agitated. He was pacing. We didn't like not knowing where our pup was. Whether she was safe.

I raised my voice to a shout. "Remy?"

What if she wasn't safe? Dammit! Where was she?

Turning, I ran from room to room, searching more thoroughly this time–opening closets and looking under the beds in case she was playing a game.

Where the fuck was my daughter?

Shit. Had someone come in and taken her? Had she walked out the front door?

"Remy Marie, if you're hiding from Daddy, I want you to come out right now. You're too good of a hider."

Nothing.

Adrenaline started to pump through me. If anyone had touched my pup, my wolf would rip them into pieces.

I went to the front door. Locked. I went to the back door. Shit. Why hadn't I noticed that it was open a few inches?

Fuck, fuck, fuck!

I flung it wide, stepped out onto the deck, and scanned the yard. It was an older neighborhood, so there were well-established trees and shrubs. Only partial fencing. I was getting a fucking full perimeter fence installed tomorrow to keep her in.

But right now I didn't know where she was. I ran a hand through my damp hair.

What if she'd gotten lost? Wandered into traffic? Had been fucking *kidnapped*?

"*Remy!*" I bellowed into the air. My voice held the deadly reverberation of a wolf in crisis. They talked about mama bears protecting their young. That was nothing compared to what a papa wolf would do if anyone so much as breathed on his pup.

"Over here, Daddy!"

Oh fate. Her little voice carried across the summer afternoon air. It came from the neighbor's yard.

Thank fuck. My wolf howled in relief. I sighed, but my heart still pounded.

I was soothed, but I was pissed because she scared the fuck out of me. I'd left her to color or watch TV when I'd showered before. She'd never left the house. Not once.

But not once were we here in this new place, either.

I bolted across the yard, ducked under a low branch on an ash tree, and weaved around a lilac bush.

There, sitting on the concrete stoop of the neighboring house's back patio, was Remy and a young woman. Giggling and laughing and eating fucking popsicles.

The young woman looked up at me with a wide, dimpled smile.

"Hi, Daddy," Remy said brightly.

JOY

LIVING IN MONTANA, the possibility of a wild animal charging through the underbrush was not uncommon. But a muscled, tattooed man wearing nothing but a tiny pink towel around his waist was a surprise.

Especially one this attractive.

Holy shit, he was good looking.

This was Remy's daddy?

He had red hair. Everywhere.

The towel did little to hide the fact because the towel was little. It was pink and had...embroidered strawberries on the ends. I guessed it was one of Remy's.

It only contrasted how big and virile he was. Six feet, sturdy frame. Muscled. Broad shouldered. Again, muscled. Abs you could climb. Yup, muscled. Thighs like tree trunks.

And beneath the towel... big there, too.

The towel might fit a four-year old girl just fine, but

EVERYTHING on this guy was either shown outright or outlined very distinctly.

My mouth watered, and the sun suddenly became even hotter than it had been. I put the popsicle in my mouth in hope of cooling off.

His gaze followed the action with a dark glower.

"Hi, Daddy!" Remy said again. She bounced a little on the stoop with her excitement. "This is Joy. We're having pops."

His daughter was so sweet. And bright. Now I knew where she got her strawberry blonde locks.

"I see that." He stomped over to us, which shouldn't be possible in bare feet, but he somehow managed it.

I had to tip my head back to keep my eyes on his and not the rest of his Adonis physique. I could even see those V things that male models had. His face softened as he squatted down in front of me, and that towel–

My eyes practically bugged out of my head at the sight of his dick. His big, thick, ridiculously-attractive-for-a-dick dick.

He must've figured out his towel wasn't working at the same time I cleared my throat. He popped back to his feet and held the knot at his hip tightly.

"Baby, you can't leave the house without me," he said gruffly.

"I didn't want to color anymore," Remy defended herself. "I heard Joy singing, so I came out. She lives here. She does clay in the garage. Wanna see?"

He frowned at me like I might have been trying to lure her into my house or something.

"She paints it and puts it in an oven. It sounds so fun! She's gonna let me do some if it's okay with you."

The dad-I'd-like-to-fuck grunted. I couldn't tell if it was a yes or a no.

For some foolish reason, his disgruntled demeanor made him all the more attractive to me. I didn't know why– maybe I found grumps a challenge or something.

I was never into guys who were charming and friendly and into *me*. I was like a cat who knew exactly which strangers weren't cat people, and expended its energy and affection on only them. Needless to say, I was *very* single because of it.

"Her hair's not red like mine," Remy continued. "It's like a princess and like spun gold in that book we read and also in that movie. What's spun gold? Does it go around and around in circles?"

The girl had energy. The popsicle perhaps wasn't the best idea, but they were all natural. Raspberry, my favorite flavor. It had two sticks, and I'd split it in half, so we shared. I'd doubted she could eat a whole one in this heat before it melted all over her. I was right because half the juice stained her face and her right hand.

"The popsicle is all-natural, no sugar added," I told him. "I'm sorry, I should have asked you first, but she said she didn't have any food allergies and that you were in the shower."

I probably shouldn't have reminded myself of that fact because the thought sent my gaze on another wander over his mostly-naked body, looking for water droplets. Wondering if he'd like a little help next time.

I could–it was definitely an option–hold the soap or something.

The man grunted. Looked at me with an intense gaze.

Took a deep breath as if trying to calm himself.

Then looked away.

I guess he was pissed about the popsicle.

Whoops.

Ignoring me, he said, "Remy, you can't run off like that. I didn't know where you were." He shot a dark look my way. "And you should never accept food from strangers."

"I'm sorry, Daddy." She tipped her freckled face up to mine. "Is Joy a stranger? I thought she was our neighbor."

He didn't answer. Instead, he said, "Time to go."

Remy jumped to her feet. "Thank you for the pop!" She dashed off back to her house.

"She's adorable." I pushed to my bare feet. It was in the high eighties, and to combat the warm-for-Montana temperatures, I had on a short sundress, and my fair hair was pulled up into a sloppy bun.

He grunted again.

I wasn't sure what else to say to a mostly naked man in my backyard who seemed disgruntled that I befriended his daughter. There was no etiquette for this.

He stared. I stared back.

Then he turned on his bare feet and left.

I got a great view of his muscular ass in the tiny towel.

Maybe I shouldn't have given his daughter a popsicle. Maybe he shouldn't have flashed me his impressive dick.

And that dick belonged to my neighbor? Wow.

The man was grumpy. Growly. Gorgeous.

And I didn't even know his name.

3

WES

I MIGHT HAVE BEEN a dick back there to my new neighbor, but I didn't really care. Hell, I didn't even want to think about flashing myself. What kind of man does that? She must think I'm a perv. And a dick.

I knew I came off as an asshole, not just to Joy, but to everyone. Even before Remy, I'd never been much for socializing. I wasn't the kind of guy to make small talk or gab around with the neighbors. The last four years of single parenting had made me downright prickly.

If I had a daily allotment of words to say, I sure as shit used them all up with Remy. She was a chatterbox. It seemed the only time she stopped talking was when she was asleep. For the rest of the world, I didn't have much left in me for chitchat or pleasantries or any of that shit. My well of patience was completely dried up.

Getting saddled—no, not *saddled*, that was the wrong

word—I fucking *adored* Remy, but I didn't expect to raise a pup from infancy all by myself. I didn't even know I had a pup until I returned to my home pack after a six-month rodeo circuit and saw her mom in town, pregnant.

Soraya hadn't been my girlfriend. She hadn't even been a friend. We'd hooked up *one time* on a full moon run. ONE TIME! She was a couple years younger than I was and had always been a wild one. Since she was eighteen, she'd run off and pop back in town when she was in trouble or needed money from her rich father. She'd just returned once again when we hooked up.

Yeah, the pull-out method obviously hadn't been enough. So Remy was an oopsie baby.

I'd found a place to live and moved Soraya in with me to do right by her and the pup. But as soon as she had Remy, Soraya left town. Popped out the baby, took one look at her, and was gone. While she may have returned to the pack again, I'd moved here to Cooper Valley to steer clear. I hadn't seen her since.

I had no regrets. Remy was everything to me.

It was just that I'd known fuck-all about raising a newborn pup, and it had been a journey to say the least. Especially when I had to take her on the road with me from competition to competition to ride bulls because that was the only way I could save enough money to buy us this place and provide for her.

I was good at it, too. Prize money came in. Sponsorships. Now we were set with a good house in a good town with a good pack.

I went inside and found Remy back in her booster

coloring, where she was supposed to have been while I was showering.

I stomped over and kissed the top of her messy redhead. "You scared me, baby."

My daughter looked up at me with wide, surprised eyes. They were green, like Soraya's. Like every time I peered into her miniature, innocent face, my chest squeezed up tight.

I loved her so much it physically hurt. The pain of fucking this up–parenting her the wrong way, or fate forbid, ever losing her–had a strangle-hold on my love.

"*You* were scared?" she asked in wonderment.

I set my hand on my bare chest. "You don't think daddies can be scared?"

"I didn't think you were scared of anything."

I pulled back a chair beside her and plunked into it. I was still wearing nothing but Remy's undersized towel. "I don't get scared for me, Remy baby. But you know what scares me a lot?"

Her little forehead crinkled. She had a red ring from the popsicle around her mouth. "What?"

I leaned in and looked into her innocent little eyes. "Thinking something might happen to you."

"But I'm okay, Daddy." She reached out and patted my hand. As if she was the one offering comfort. "Joy is my friend."

Joy. That was the neighbor.

I considered Remy, biting back my automatic response, which would be to tell her not to trust strangers or whatever bullshit parents were supposed to say these days. I'd picked this town, this house, because of how safe it was.

How she could go and visit neighbors and play with other kids on the block.

I cocked my head. "How do you know she's a friend?"

Remy returned to coloring, dragging an orange crayon up and down over a stick figure like she was giving it clothes. "She smells good."

For some reason, that made goosebumps rise on my arms.

She smells good.

"You were trusting your wolf instincts." I gave her a nod. Parenting was a little at a time kind of guidance.

Wolf pups didn't shift until puberty, and some packs—especially those in cities or more integrated with humans—didn't teach their pups what they were until they were old enough to honor the pack secret.

But I'd had to explain to Remy when we were on the rodeo circuit that I couldn't be hurt by the bulls because I was a wolf. The animals had scared her, and that helped her watch me without crying every time I let myself get thrown to make it seem realistic. More than that, though, I believed it was important to teach her to listen to her wolf instincts. To differentiate between her animal side and her little girl side. I didn't know anything about being female, so I was trying my best.

It was true that I had to be careful Remy didn't say the wrong thing to a human, but I wanted my daughter to know what she was. I was proud of her. Proud of what she was and what she'd become. I'd taught her to distinguish the scent of a human from a wolf. She already knew she could talk freely about what she was in front of wolves, but had to keep our secret from humans.

"Yeah, I know she's a human, but she's the good kind." Remy kept coloring, trading out the orange crayon for a yellow one, which she used to scratch a ball of color over the stick figure's head.

I scrubbed a hand over my beard. "What's the good kind?"

"The kind like Joy."

Kids said the damnedest things. In my mind, I returned to the neighbor's back stoop. I'd been wrapped up in the relief of finding Remy and the agitation of unused adrenaline, so I hadn't paid enough attention to the woman. Specifically, since Remy mentioned it, the way she smelled.

But Remy was right. It had been pleasant.

Sweet and warm, like fresh-baked donuts. Like honey vanilla caramels, too gooey to eat.

But now that I recalled it, her scent had only further agitated me. Like, it irritated me that my wolf had found her scent pleasing. It made me cranky. Or *crankier*.

I remembered the way her gaze had gone to my dick when I squatted down. That had been a dumb move, but I wasn't modest. Not that I'd planned to flash my neighbor wearing only my four-year-old's tiny fucking towel.

A flush had spread across her chest, but she hadn't looked embarrassed.

No, there had been a boldness in the way she looked at me. Like she'd been drinking me in.

Like she was interested. Like she wanted me.

I scrubbed a hand over the back of my neck, which seemed to heat with the thought. Because for some reason, I was glad she'd been interested. That she found my body appealing.

Joy. The neighbor. Pretty blonde hair all messy on top of her head. Blue eyes, full lips that seemed to be in a perpetual smile.

I wasn't interested, but I should have shaken her hand instead of showing her my dick. Then I'd have her scent on my palm to review now. I could have introduced myself.

I'd just bought the house next to her and had a preschooler who I apparently couldn't trust to stay in the house when I told her to.

She might be someone I could ask to babysit now and again. Like, if I had to run to the grocery store after bedtime. Hell, I'd been worried about what I was going to do with Remy after her morning preschool during the summer calving season, which would be starting up any day now.

This was my first season as foreman. I'd missed the spring calving. So while I was in charge, I was winging it a bit based on what this ranch did with their cattle. I figured if I had to go to the ranch at night, I'd pull her out of bed and make a little nest of blankets for her to sleep in my pickup while I worked.

Once she was asleep, she didn't wake up for anything.

But if I had a neighbor who didn't mind coming over...

My thoughts had nothing to do with the fact that Joy was young and pretty. She wasn't my type. The last thing I needed was a sweet, dimpled, blue-eyed human in my life, except as a babysitter.

Nope.

My heart was closed to females–she-wolves and humans alike. It couldn't contain the pressure of loving a four-year-old pup. Plus, I didn't have enough time to manage one tiny female and myself. There was no way I was going to complicate things by getting involved with a woman. Especially a human.

Not even one that smelled like pralines and sunshine.

"Is that Joy?" I tapped the paper Remy was drawing on.

She nodded her head, her red curls bobbing. "Uh huh. You can tell by the bun on top." She pointed to the yellow ball above the stick figure's head. "How do you write her name?"

"Let's sound it out," I said, taking a cue from Remy's preschool teacher, Riley. "J-J-J."

She stuck her tongue into the corner of her mouth, just like she always did when concentrating. "G?"

"J. But you're right, G makes that sound, too."

Remy's face scrunched up as she drew a giant letter J at the top of the paper in yellow. She traded out the yellow crayon for a blue one. "And then what?"

"Oh-oh-oh." I made the sound with my mouth.

She glanced at me for confirmation as she drew an O beside the J.

I nodded.

"Is that all?"

"Y. Like in Remy." I hoped she wouldn't ask why it wasn't pronounced *Joey*, then, because I sure as hell didn't know. I didn't think they taught exceptions to sounding things out quite yet.

When she'd added her crooked Y, she held it up. "Can I bring it to her?"

My dick twitched under the towel at the thought of returning next door. Which was exactly why I had to say no.

"Not now." I stood and ruffled Remy's hair. "Daddy has to get dressed and figure out something for you to eat for dinner."

"Can we buy popsicles?" Remy asked.

An image of Joy licking her raspberry popsicle flashed through my mind. That tongue dragging up the side as she perused my body with her leisurely gaze.

Suddenly, my mouth watered, and it wasn't for popsicles.

Maybe I should be neighborly. I could bring Remy over to deliver the drawing. I could introduce myself properly and get off on a better foot with my new neighbor. After I got dressed.

More importantly, I could get another good whiff of her scent.

That would be the only reason for going over there. Not because I was interested.

I definitely didn't want Joy to lick my popsicle. Or to open those thighs for me to get my face between them.

I wasn't wondering whether the scent of her arousal smelled as sweet as the rest of her.

Nor what sounds she'd made when she got excited.

Nope. Not going there. You didn't screw your neighbor. That had to be a fucking rule, right?

Especially not when she was a human, and I was a single parent and a wolf.

4

JOY

I SAT on my low stool, knees spread wide around my potter's wheel. My right foot was on the pedal, which adjusted how fast it circled. My hands were covered in wet clay up past my wrists. My old apron covered my tank top and shorts from the splatter, but my knees and a few spots on my thighs weren't so lucky.

Being messy was part of the job as a potter. I took a cube of wet clay and turned it into functional objects, like plates and mugs and vases. A vase was what I was making now.

I dipped the wet sponge in the water bucket, squeezed it out, then set it right where the wheel and clay met. It looked like a vase, about a foot tall, but I needed to taper in the bottom. I pressed in as the vase spun round and round. Slowly, with consistent pressure, it narrowed.

I dunked the sponge and did it again and again until I

was satisfied. Then I grabbed a small wooden tool to remove the excess.

A spiral ribbon of clay came free. I tossed it into the little pile of excess clay that was slowly growing.

The music was on low. The garage door was raised. It was a gorgeous Montana day.

But it was still hot. Sweat dotted my brow, and I couldn't touch it to wipe it away. I'd learned that the hard way long ago when I used to get covered head to toe in clay.

Taking my foot off the pedal, the vase slowed, then stopped.

I eyed it critically. This was a new direction I was going. The first two I'd delivered to the craft shop in town had sold the first week. I'd sent a few to shops around the country that sold my work. This one was headed to Texas when it was complete.

Grabbing the wire with the little wood dowel pieces on either end, I slid it under the bottom of the wet vase to separate it from the wheel.

Checking to make sure I had a place to set it on the shelf to dry, I glanced over my shoulder. It was then my cell rang.

"Shit."

Carefully, I picked up the vase and went across the garage and set it down.

Pushing out my bottom lip, I blew air up and over my face, blowing my wayward strands of hair out of my eyes.

I couldn't grab my cell—which was still ringing—but I used my pinky to swipe up, leaving only a small smear on the glass. With the speaker button on, I could talk hands free.

"It's a joyful day!"

"Hi Joy, this is Joann at Segal Crafts."

Her store in Oregon had sold a few pieces of mine. I even sent her one last week.

"Oh, hi! I was just working on the next vase."

"That's great. I'm calling with bad news, though."

That didn't sound good.

"The box you sent. Everything in it was broken."

"What?" Everything? There were... fourteen mugs, three serving dishes and one vase. I was an expert at packing breakables, but things did happen. Still. Everything?

"You should definitely take it up with the delivery service and claim the insurance on it. I have photos I can email you to add to the claim."

It was five hundred dollars worth of goods.

I could probably get an insurance check as she mentioned, but it took time. I'd done it before. This was a lot! I needed that money. I'd hoped Joann was calling to tell me she'd paid me electronically, and I'd have what I needed to pay the mortgage.

Now?

"Well, shoot. Yes, of course I'll take those photos from you. Do you, um, want replacements?"

Please want replacements!

"It will take at least a week to make them all from start to finish."

After the items were thrown on the wheel, they had to dry fully before they could be fired in my kiln or the water inside made the item explode. Then they were glazed, then fired again.

Pottery wasn't a quick art.

"Yes, please. Everyone loves your work."

I quietly exhaled in relief.

Sure, I'd lose money from the extra clay and paints doing them all over. And the time it took for redoing the order, I could be making something else. She was a solid client and a nice person. It wasn't her fault.

"Thank you for calling," I said. "I'll let you know when replacements will be done."

"Take care, Joy." Joann ended the call.

I stared at my space. I'd bought this fixer-upper a few years ago for the detached garage specifically. It was the perfect potter's studio. When I first moved in, I'd ensured the wiring in here was up to code before I fixed the leaky faucet in the kitchen. I even had the fire department come out and confirm everything was safe for the kiln.

The house was *still* a fixer-upper. It needed a lot of work. Unlike Remy and her father's house next door that had been modernized from top to bottom. I knew the old neighbors and had seen all the updates they'd done to the place.

Someday. My sink wasn't dripping any longer, but the windows needed replacing, the furnace upgraded, and the tile in the bathroom shouldn't be avocado green. I'd get to it all eventually. If I had the extra money to tackle those projects. I wasn't broke, but I was definitely just keeping my head above water.

My pieces were starting to sell around the country, and money was coming in, but setbacks seemed to consistently pop up and, well, set me back.

One pot ahead, two pots back, or however the saying went.

My cell chimed again. This time with a text.

The name on the screen made me smile. Marina. My friend from yoga class.

Colton's out. Come over. I've got wine.

She had me at *come over*, but wine, too? Boy, did I need a glass. Or two.

I pushed the speech-to-text button because there was no way I could type with my filthy hands.

I'm in. Give me an hour.

JOY

"–AND it wasn't sugar... it was salt!" Marina exclaimed.

I couldn't help but giggle, imagining her client eating a cake that tasted so bad.

We were behind the main house at Wolf Ranch. The lawn had lounge chairs with thick cushions on them that faced the barn and the fields beyond. It was a pretty spot. The sun was low on the horizon, glinting through the trees.

Marina lived here with her man, Colton, along with Colton's brother, Rob, and his wife Willow. There was a bunkhouse down by the barn, which had a rotating group of ranch hands living in it. I heard the only people staying there now were Johnny and his wife Emma.

"If you're not throwing pottery, what have you been up to? It feels like it's been ages since we got together last." She held up a finger. "In fact, it was snowing. Remember, Colton had to pick me up from your place."

I nodded. "I do. That was a storm."

She leaned over with the wine bottle and refilled my glass.

"As for what I've been up to, work," I told her. "Work. And more work."

I'd already told her about the broken shipment.

"Spending all your time in your garage isn't fun."

I shrugged. "It's not a garage, it's my studio. You stay inside in your kitchen to bake."

She waggled her eyebrows. "I have Colton to carry me out of there and get me to do other things."

I grinned. I could only imagine *how* he carried her–probably over his shoulder–and what those *other things* were.

"I love that you have Colton," I said with a sigh.

"We need to get you a man."

Instantly, I thought of Mr. Towel, my neighbor. Now he was *all* man.

I'd gone to bed the night before thinking of him. Heck, I'd even seen his dick, and we hadn't even gone on a date! I knew the man was packing. Knew he was gorgeous. Literally every inch of him. Despite his apparent grouchiness, I knew he was kind to his daughter. Protective. Bossy.

I'd touched myself thinking of him, minus the towel.

How he'd growl and boss *me* around.

How I'd like it. How I'd come when he ordered me to do so.

How–

"Earth to Joy. Where'd you go, and can I get a ticket to join you?" she asked.

I sighed. "Sorry. I was thinking about my new neighbor."

"Oh?" She looked intrigued. "Good or bad?"

"Good. *Very* good."

As if talking about him, I conjured him up.

Because I could swear my new neighbor just came out of the barn. It wasn't that close, so maybe I needed glasses, but I would recognize that stellar form anywhere. And then–

It *was* him! Because galloping like a pretend horse right behind him was a little girl.

"Him." I pointed.

Marina whipped her head around.

"Wes?" she gasped. "He's your new neighbor? Seriously?"

Wes. I never got his name.

I nodded. "You can't miss the red hair."

"Oh my gosh, he's gorgeous. I know I've got Colton, and he's perfect, but I'm not blind. If you're into a grumpy ginger guy, he's it."

"Is he... mean?" I asked, thinking of little Remy. She was sweet and bright, and I didn't want anyone to be unkind to her, especially her dad.

"Mean?" She laughed. "Nooooo. Aloof. Standoffish. Not shy. Introverted. Heck, he's just plain grumpy. But look at him with his daughter. See if that doesn't make your heart melt like butter."

He was tossing her up onto his back and pretending to be a horse. I could hear her giggling from here.

"So where's Remy's mom?"

"Deadbeat," she muttered with a wave of her hand.

"She abandoned the baby right after she was born, from what I can gather. I suspect that's why he's so grumpy. He was single-dad-ing it on the rodeo circuit for three and half years, if you can believe it."

"He was in the rodeo?" I squeaked, my mind going to even hotter places. That guy on the back of a bull?

"Yup." Marina fanned herself then laughed.

"He took her all over the country? Are you serious?" I stared out at the pair of them before they disappeared back into the barn. "How did *that* work?"

"I don't know—not too well. I mean, the rodeo pays well, and I guess he was saving up to be able to buy that house next to you, but the circuit is hardly the place for a baby or toddler."

I shook my head. "I can't imagine. So how did he end up here? Through Boyd?"

Everyone in Cooper Valley knew Boyd Wolf had been a rodeo star before he met his wife, Audrey, and retired from the circuit.

Marina took a sip of her wine and nodded. "Exactly. Boyd saw Wes last time the rodeo was in town, and when he found out Wes had a four-year-old on the road with him, he offered him a foreman position here. I think he and Rob sort of made the job up for him because it's not like Boyd or Colton couldn't do that work."

My heart melted even more. Not only was Wes a hero for going it alone as a dad on the road, but the entire Wolf clan were heroes for caring enough about his kid to create a well-paying position for him to get him off the back of a bull. That couldn't be safe.

"He's not much of a talker, but I pried out of him that

even though the money was good, he was relieved to quit because he knew it was time for Remy to go to preschool and interact with other kids."

"He sounds like a stand-up guy."

Marina turned her gaze to me. With her dark hair, her eyes were striking. "Honey, he's a good one. Rob wouldn't have hired him if he wasn't. He wouldn't have lasted a day, and you know that."

All of the men at Wolf Ranch were nice. Attentive to their women. Big and brawny. Perhaps a little intimidating, but she was right. They wouldn't let some dick work here.

"No girlfriend?" I grinned at Marina. "You know. Asking for a friend."

She smiled back. "No girlfriend. He hasn't dated anyone since he's been here, that I know of. I think Remy takes all his focus, but you never know. That could change when he meets the gorgeous girl next door." She stood. "Come on, you want me to introduce you?"

I gave her a wry grin and stayed sitting where I was. "We've met. And honestly, he didn't seem all that impressed at our first meeting."

Me, though? I was *very* impressed with what I saw of him.

Marina waved a dismissive hand. "Well, like I said, he's grumpy. Don't let that deter you."

Deter? Maybe help instead.

6

WES

THUNDER BOOMED, shaking the walls of the house just a split second after the flash of lightning.

It'd been brewing for about ten minutes now. This time, the electricity went out.

Fuck.

I headed to the kitchen wearing nothing but a pair of pajama pants to find a candle in case Remy woke up to use the bathroom. I had one in a glass jar somewhere. Candles weren't my thing, but Remy had begged me to buy it from the dollar store last week.

There. I found the candle and lit it. It was scent-free, so at least I didn't have to deal with a synthetic smell driving my wolf nuts.

I set it on the kitchen table as a nightlight of sorts. Fortunately, Remy usually slept like the dead once I got her to sleep. If the storm had been going when I was trying to put her to bed, she would've been too scared, but she hadn't yet stirred.

I found myself glancing through the back sliding glass door toward the house next door. Wondered if Joy was okay.

That was stupid. My neighbor was a grown woman. She wouldn't be afraid of a summer storm.

Still, the wind whistled through the air vents and whipped tree branches against the house. I could hear the loud thump of one hitting the side of her house. The protective part of me wondered if she needed anything. She was human and, therefore, vulnerable to danger.

But what kind of danger was I worried about? It wasn't like the wind was going to blow her house down. The chances of lightning striking her roof were pretty slim with taller trees around.

I was the big bad wolf. I knew all about this.

She was fine.

If she was scared, that wasn't my problem. I wasn't about to go rushing next door to hold her and tell her she was safe. That job could be reserved for some other guy.

Except the thought of holding her landed in a visceral way. It landed as pleasure. Like my wolf wanted the little human next door scared and shaking in my arms. Turning to me for comfort.

Which was fucking crazy.

Still, the idea of some other guy offering that comfort set my teeth on edge. No fucking way. But that was just because I didn't like the idea of having strange men near my house. Not when I had a little girl here.

I wasn't jealous at the thought of some random would-be comforter to my neighbor. I was just being a protective dad.

Yeah, that was it. I ran a hand down my face and sighed.

Rain beat against the windows and roof. Lightning flashed again at the same time the thunder boomed.

My wolf let out an instinctive growl, ready to protect and defend my family against the storm. I cut through the house and peeked in on Remy. I didn't need a candle with my wolf eyesight to see her tucked beneath her lavender comforter, her hand thrown up over her head.

The wind gusted, making my windows rattle. All of a sudden, I heard a loud crack and the sound of shattered glass.

A female screamed.

Joy.

Fuck. What had happened?

One last look at Remy ensured she was out cold, and I bolted across the house and threw open the sliding door. It was pitch black outside, but my wolf eyes adjusted to the dark as I sprinted next door. The heavy rain pelted my face.

I was headed to her house once again soaking wet.

"Holy fuck!"

An entire tree–one that had been in her backyard–had blown over and landed on Joy's roof. The roof and part of the adjacent wall had caved in, smashing the glass to her window. A huge tree limb was half in, half out of her house.

Fuck!

"Joy?" I shouted at the same time thunder cracked again.

She wouldn't hear me. She was human. She could be hurt.

I didn't run around to knock on her door. Didn't wait for permission or an invitation.

Fuck that.

I just leaped straight through her broken window, scaling the tree limb to get there. When I kicked the broken glass in to get through, Joy's scream sounded just below me and to the right.

"Oh fuck!" I plunged through the broken window, landing in a pile of debris on a bed. "Joy?"

She was under the rubble, pushing her way out.

Fate, no.

"Joy!" I lunged for her, hurling the broken sheets of drywall that had come down from her ceiling out of the way to get to her. The tree limb wasn't moving as easily, but it didn't pin her, thank fuck.

She scrambled off the bed, landing in the tiny space between it and the wall. "Oh, my God! What happened?"

Rain came in along with the wind, which whipped her curtains around.

Fate. Had she been...*on the bed* when the ceiling caved in on her?

I jumped off it and yanked it toward me and onto its side, so I could get to her. I forgot not to show her my superhuman strength. Forgot everything but getting to my fragile neighbor before she was badly hurt. Maybe she already was, and I didn't know it yet.

She could be cut. Bleeding. Worse.

"Joy, come here." I snatched her up, carrying her out of the bedroom and away from the collapsing roof.

Her arms came around my shoulders, and my wolf calmed

down. I got a clean hit of her honey scent, and lightning struck again–this time inside my body. It was like all my cells woke up at the same time. I became electrified. A switch turned on.

Fuck, she smelled good.

She smelled...*right.*

I never thought anyone–human or wolf–smelled wrong, but this was *right.*

I suddenly found it impossible to swallow.

Equally impossible was putting Joy down. She wasn't safe here, in this broken house. We were both soaking wet and covered in plaster and debris. Worse, she might be concussed or cut and bleeding.

I needed to get her to my place to look her over. No way were we staying here.

Without saying a word–not unusual for me–I stomped out her back door in my bare feet and carried Joy in through mine. I picked up the lit candle from the kitchen table on the way to my bathroom. I only paused to peek in on Remy, who was still sleeping and was missing all of this. Then, I lowered Joy gently to her feet and set the candle on the vanity to start picking chunks of wood and plaster from her hair. I kept one hand on her elbow because her legs seemed unsteady.

"A... a tree fell on my roof." Joy was clearly in shock, still trying to assimilate what had just happened.

I wasn't one for extraneous words, but I forced one out because the situation called for a response. She deserved my response. "Yeah."

"My roof is... My house..." She appeared dazed.

"Are you hurt?" I raked a gaze over her. Her blonde hair

was soaked and sticking to her face, covered in the white powder of plaster from the ceiling. Her arms and legs were covered in more debris that hadn't washed off in the rain. Her pajamas were tiny sleep shorts and a snug camisole. Neither hid her lush shape. The fact that they were both wet through meant I could see her nipples. Every bump. I knew their size. Their color.

My mouth watered for a taste. Lower, the material clung to her folds.

Holy hell was she perfection. My wolf wanted to fuck her right here and now, but I had enough brain function left–since all my blood had dropped to my dick–to know this wasn't the time.

She examined her body along with me. Her hand came up to rub a spot on her forehead where a lump was forming and winced.

"Looks like a bruise there." Gently, I pushed her wet hair out of her face to examine it. "Where else does it hurt?" I softened my voice like I would if I were talking to Remy after she took a spill. I turned her chin from side to side to examine for other bruises and ran my fingertips around the back of her head. "Do you know your name? Your birthday?" I tried to remember the things the rodeo doctors would ask us after we had a fall.

She let out a semi-hysterical laugh. "Yes. Joy Wallace. March thirteenth."

"Okay." I continued to scan her. She didn't appear to have any broken bones or open cuts that I could see although it was really hard to notice when my eyes kept returning to her nipples.

"I'm Wes," I remembered to offer, since I hadn't introduced myself to her the day before. "Weston Sparks."

"I know. I'm friends with Marina at Wolf Ranch. I was actually over there last night and saw you guys. Oh, is Remy okay?"

"Yes. Sleeping right through it all."

She turned her head in the direction of her house as if still trying to assimilate what happened. "You came in through my window?"

I nodded. "Yeah. I heard the crash. Were you in bed when it happened?"

"I was trying to sleep, but the thunder woke me up. And then suddenly, the ceiling fell on my face."

"Of all the places the tree could fall–" My voice grew rough with a ferocious need to run back and protect her all over again. Thinking of what could've happened if she'd been crushed beneath the weight of the roof made my wolf crazy. It was a fucking miracle she was mostly unscathed.

"It's...it's raining in my house right now."

"I know. There's nothing we can do tonight. I pushed the bed out of the way, so there's nothing under the hole."

She nodded. "Thank you." Her voice was soft and sincere.

Fate. Something about the way she said those two words made my throat constrict. Like it meant something to her. Hell, I was wrong about not needing to be the one to comfort her because right now, I sure as fuck did.

"I should have seen it coming," I said, wanting to punch my own face in. Fuck, I'd stood in my kitchen and purposely decided *not* to check on her. "I heard a branch hitting your house, but I never thought–"

"How could anyone see it coming?" Her voice held that hysterical laughter again.

I had most of the rubble picked off her now. A fresh urge—a darker urge—began to war with my need to take care of her now that I'd accomplished that.

I cleared my throat. "Do you want to shower the rest of the mess off?" I tried not to picture myself peeling her out of her cute, very wet pajamas. Stepping into the shower with her and handing her the soap. No, using it myself on her. Checking over every inch of her to make sure she wasn't hurt. No, *licking.*

"Yes." Her voice sounded rusty, too. "Um, that sounds good."

Right. *Move, Wes. Don't just stand there staring at your beautiful neighbor.*

I threw open the cabinet and pulled out a folded towel. At least I'd gotten most things put in place by now and had a grown-up towel to offer her. Although I wouldn't mind seeing her in just a skimpy towel. And if she wanted to flash me her pussy?

I cleared my throat. "Here you go. I'll make some hot cocoa."

Cocoa? Why did I offer that? She wasn't four years old.

"Or tea? Hell, whiskey?"

She rewarded me with a wobbly smile. "Cocoa sounds heavenly."

Okay, I wasn't too off base. I leaned past her to turn on the hot water in the shower then forced myself to leave.

As I stood outside the bathroom door listening to make sure she was okay—that she wasn't going to pass out and hit her head—I tried not to imagine what she'd look like naked.

I didn't let myself wonder if her skin tasted as sweet as it smelled.

There was no room in my life for a female.

Besides, everyone knew the human rule—*you don't date your neighbor.*

But I wasn't human, my wolf was telling me.

7

JOY

I STOOD under the hot spray of water. I was still in shock, I had to be. My hands shook as I ran my palms over my arms to rinse off the grit. I felt disconnected from my body. A little spacey.

There were thoughts in my head, but they flitted in and out without connecting.

I forced myself to review what had happened to bring myself back to reality.

I'd been sleeping, but the storm woke me. I'd looked at the clock beside my bed, but it had been dark, so the power must've gone out.

Right. How had I not noticed? The power was out at this house, too. That explained why I was showering by candlelight in my hot neighbor's bathroom. Duh.

Wait.

Oh my gawd! Wes. He'd been such a hero.

I went over it all again, picking up where I left off. The ceiling had caved in on me. A loud crash. Drywall falling. Wetness. I screamed. Then I was shoving heavy boards and plaster off of me and climbing out of bed. Suddenly, a giant man came through my window. Dressed in nothing but a pair of pajama pants.

He'd flipped my bed on its side like the Incredible Hulk.

I didn't consider myself the damsel in distress type, but that? Epic. And yeah, it definitely made my hot neighbor even more attractive. Was that even possible?

Naked with a kiddie towel, then leaping through broken windows in PJ pants?

Marina was right—he was gruff but kind. Fierce. Protective and concerned.

I felt safe in his house. I felt cared for in his shower. For once, someone was looking out for me, and it felt... good.

By the time I finished showering, the shaking was subsiding. Still, I felt off. I had the sense of something big being caught in my chest or my throat. Like somehow, the storm had entered my body, and now I needed a good cry to let it all out.

I turned off the water and toweled myself dry.

There was no wearing the pajamas I'd had on. They were soaking wet and filthy.

A light tap sounded on the door, and the handle turned. Wes' hand, followed by a strong muscular forearm, slipped through the crack in the door, holding a flannel shirt. "Here. Uh, if you need something to wear."

I let out a croaking laugh and took the shirt. He must've been listening for the water to turn off, waiting to give it to me. "I do. Thank you." The fabric was soft and worn. Lifting it to my nose, I sniffed the flannel.

Spicy and dark. Manly. Just like Wes.

I liked that it was his. I slipped my arms through the sleeves, and it fell over my shoulders like a warm blanket. Draped long down to mid-thigh, and I had to roll up the sleeves.

I opened the door, and the candlelight cast on Wes standing in the hallway. He was leaning against the wall opposite, one hand rubbing the back of his neck like he wasn't sure of his next move. He'd dried off and changed, too, into a different pair of pajama pants. His tattoos were once again on full display.

"You okay?" he wondered. It was dark, the candlelight giving off enough glow for me to see his gaze raked down my body, as if checking again to make sure I wasn't hurt.

Something bad had happened, but I wasn't going through it alone. I wasn't stuck in the mess. I was safe and could deal with the problems that would arise tomorrow. I didn't have to be upbeat and smiling. I didn't have to be strong in this moment.

Gah. It was because of that that his two words made tears spring to my eyes. While I did need to somehow get this energy out, crying was the last thing I wanted to do with my neighbor. Crying never solved anything. I wasn't hurt. I was fine. Whole.

I ducked my head. "I just...I think I'm twitchy from the adrenaline in my system and... yeah, I feel like I need to run a marathon or something."

"You need to get it out," he said, as if it was a poison.

I looked up. "What?"

"The excess adrenaline. Otherwise you'll crash."

Get it out. Exactly. I needed to get rid of this excess adrenaline. Suddenly, I knew just what I needed to do.

I acted on impulse. My brain was too short-circuited to overthink at the moment. I just stepped right up to Wes and pulled his face down to mine.

Our mouths collided. I was forceful. Aggressive. I put some tongue into it.

His arm looped around my lower back, and the unbuttoned shirt he gave me to wear fell open, baring me to him. But he reared back, breaking the kiss. "Whoa."

I instantly released my arms from his neck, licked my lips. "Sorry." I started to turn away, but he used the arm at my waist to keep me in place. "Sorry, I just–"

He studied my face, the flicker of candlelight making the harsh lines of his jaw look even stronger.

"–I just needed to blow off some steam. Like you said."

"I got you."

"What about Remy?" I asked, glancing over my shoulder down the hall. "She's still okay?"

He grinned. "Still sleeping through everything. If she can sleep through a storm like this, she can sleep through me fucking you good and hard."

Yes. I wanted to be fucked good and hard. Wes. Over me. In me. Not holding back.

"I know what you need," he added, stepping into my space.

He answered with his lips. A counter-attack–just as forceful as mine had been. And then some. When his hand went to my bare butt and lifted, I wrapped my legs around his waist, and he carried me into his bedroom.

I wanted Wes. I wanted this. I needed it.

8

WES

FUCK YES, she tasted good. As good as her scent that was rubbing all over my skin.

My wolf was practically howling with satisfaction.

My dick was hard as a fucking hammer.

Joy's ass was a handful. Lush and full. Her breasts pressed against my chest, and I could feel her hard little nipples.

She was ravenous for me. Her mouth met mine with equal intensity. Her hands roamed over my bare back, my chest, and my skin lit up everywhere they went.

After I kicked the door shut behind us, I lowered her onto the bed, only breaking the kiss when it wasn't enough. I needed to taste the rest of her.

My mouth moved to her jaw, her neck. I felt her frantic pulse beneath my lips.

Then I moved lower. Her collarbone.

While her arms were in my flannel I'd given her to put on, it did nothing to cover her. She was bare to me.

I took one nipple into my mouth and sucked. Hard. With my hand, I played with the neglected one. Tugging on it. Testing her to see how she liked it. Did she like it gentle, or was there a wild thing inside of her?

I had a feeling I knew the answer because she gasped at the rough play. Squirmed. *Moaned.*

I switched sides.

She began to thrash, her hands tunneling through my hair.

"Wes," she moaned.

I moved lower, circled her navel with my tongue. Then dropped to the floor. With an easy tug on her ankles, I pulled her to me, then hooked my arms around her thighs.

Her scent was stronger here. Her pussy was open and ripe and wet now, and not from the shower or the rain storm.

I ran one blunt fingertip through her slit, coating it in her sweet juice. Put it in my mouth.

Fuck me, she tasted good. So fucking sweet. Pre-cum spurted from my dick with my need to get in her. To be coated in it.

"This all for me, honey?"

"Honey?" Her voice was breathy.

"That's what you taste like. Honey. Sticky and delicious." I dragged my tongue through her juices again. "Here's what's gonna happen. I'm going to lick this pussy until you come all over my face. Then I'm going to fuck you."

"I'm ready." She looked down her body at me. Her tits heaved with each breath.

"For my dick? You haven't even seen it yet to know what you're in for. Gotta get you ready for me."

Her lips spread in a slow smile. "I got a preview yesterday," she reminded.

"Honey, I wasn't hard then."

Her eyes flared with understanding. What she'd seen wasn't what I was going to give her now. "Show me."

I let go of her thighs and stood between her parted knees. Pushed my pajama pants down, and they dropped to my feet.

Gripping the base, I stroked my dick from root to tip. It took a while because I was big. Real big. Women I'd been with in the past took me, but it hadn't been easy. They needed to like it rough. They needed to like it deep. They needed to... hell, be okay with not walking right the next day.

"Oh my." Joy licked her lips.

She scrambled up and was on her hands and knees for me. Then her tongue flicked the tip.

"Fuck," I growled and spurted some pre-cum on her lips. Definitely wild.

Her gaze lifted to mine and seeing her mouth an inch from my dick? I was going to come just like this.

"No. Bad girl." I reached over and spanked her ass. It wasn't all that hard of a swat, but the crack of it filled the room.

She whined. "But it's so big, and I want it in my mouth, and I want to taste it–"

She had to stop talking. I couldn't handle more of what

she wanted to do with her mouth and my dick. Maybe putting it in her mouth would shut her up.

But no.

No. I needed to taste her. To make her come with my face between her thighs. I needed to somehow embed her scent onto my skin. All over my beard.

"If you want to take my dick down your throat, you can do that later. When your pussy's sore from being railed and needs some time to recover. If you keep being a bad girl, I can also fuck that ass."

Her mouth snapped shut, but she didn't blush or tell me no. In fact, she squirmed, and my wolf sense of smell picked up a big hit of arousal.

She liked those ideas. She liked me talking dirty. Taking control. Handling her.

Perhaps even being a *bad girl.* Maybe even taking her ass someday.

"For now, honey, you do what you're told."

Grabbing her by the armpits, I lifted her and tossed her onto her back. She gasped, but she also giggled. I manhandled her back into position and held onto her nice and tight, so she couldn't move. Oh, I'd let her up if she really wanted it, but she didn't. I knew it. Somehow, I knew what she needed. I held her, so she could barely squirm when I put my mouth on her pussy and ate her the fuck out.

9

JOY

HOLY SHIT.

HOLY SHIT.

This wasn't sex. It couldn't be. I'd been doing it wrong. With the wrong people.

Because Wes. God. His mouth. His hands. His body. His dick. His *dirty talk*.

All glorious.

He was just as bossy in bed as out. Actually, he hadn't gotten in bed yet. He was on his knees on the floor and had given me two orgasms already. That was just with his mouth and tongue. Now he slipped a finger inside me as his tongue did things to my clit I didn't know was possible.

One finger. Then two. Then three. Deep. Curling. Stretching.

All I could do was lie there and take it.

Because Mr. Bossy said so.

And my pussy LOVED it.

The third orgasm rippled through me, making me sweaty and wilted.

But Wes wasn't done. That was only the first part of what he'd said he had planned.

Next up... railing.

He picked me up as if I weighed no more than a feather–and wasn't the *big girl* I'd often been called–and settled me, so my head was on the pillows.

Now... finally, he climbed over me.

"Hands on the headboard." He took one of my wrists in his and raised it overhead. His touch was gentle, even though the reason for me gripping the wooden slats was because he wasn't planning on being gentle for long.

I raised my other arm and wrapped my fingers around the solid wood.

Then he sat back on his heels between my spread thighs and stroked himself. As if he was taunting me. Next up, reaching for the drawer of the bedside table. "I'm gonna wear protection for you, honey, but I want you to know I'm clean."

"I'm on the pill," I told him.

He looked to me for a moment as if he was considering. Only a moment because he tossed the condom over his shoulder, and it hit the wall. "In that case, I'm going bareback."

I smiled. This guy was all cowboy, and I freaking *loved* it.

"You ready for this?"

I nodded. "Yes. Please. I need it."

"That's right, you do."

He set a hand by my head, moved over me, and nudged my entrance.

"Take me like a good girl."

Then he filled me. Not slowly, but in one hard thrust.

"Wes!" I cried as my back arched. His gaze was on mine. Watching. Holding still.

I had to squirm to adjust, my inner walls rippling to accommodate. He was big. Deep. He'd been right; if he hadn't prepped me with those orgasms and the fingering, I might've been wet, but it would have been too much.

He knew. *He knew.*

Now? It was a lot, but it was amazing. Especially when he slowly pulled back, then thrust deep again.

Once. Then again. Then again, until it was a frantic pace. Our bodies slapped together. Our breaths mingled. I held tight to the headboard to keep from moving.

This was what I needed to get the storm out of my chest. This was being fucked.

"Holy shit."

Then he stopped, buried deep.

I had a second to wonder why, but then he rolled us, so I was on top. Now he was propped against the headboard, mostly sitting up. I was in the crook between his chest and his bent knees.

"Oh," I said, as his dick went even deeper inside me. I set my hands on his chest then leaned in and kissed him.

I couldn't hold still. I had to move. I squirmed as our tongues tangled, but when I tried to lift up, I had to sit back.

His hands went to my hips, and he helped me set a

rhythm. Up, down, circle. My clit got rubbed against his base, and I was close again.

Wes *knew* and began to lift me and drop me. His hips rocked up to meet me.

"That's it. Fuck yourself on my dick. Every inch, honey, you're getting every inch. It's all for you."

My breasts bounced. My head fell back. I just felt as we fucked.

Sweaty. Dirty.

Perfect.

When I came again, I felt myself get wetter. I cried out and kept moving to follow the pleasure. Wes' grip tightened, and he thrust deep. Held and growled.

Literally growled. I felt the rumble of it beneath my hands on his chest.

I felt how his dick thickened just before the hot spurts of his cum filled me.

I slumped onto him, and he wrapped his arms around me. I could feel his heart beating. Feel his heat. His strength.

The sounds of the storm came back to me. The howling wind. The rain. A distant roll of thunder.

But the storm was no longer inside me.

I didn't feel the tears clogging my throat anymore. Or the pressure of trapped fight or flight urges flapping like birds in my chest.

Wes slumped down, so we were settled in bed and threw the covers over us. We were still connected as he kissed the top of my head.

"Better?"

"Much," I murmured.

"I made hot cocoa—gotta love a gas stove in a storm—when you were in the shower. Still want it?"

My eyes were already closed. "No, I'm good."

Here in Wes' arms, in his bed, I felt safe.

I felt... railed. I was definitely going to be walking funny tomorrow.

I smiled as I drifted into dreamland.

10

WES

I SLID out of bed at dawn before Remy was up and stared down at the sleeping beauty in my bed. Joy's long blonde hair spilled across my pillow. It, indeed, was like the spun gold of Remy's fairytales. The color of summer sun. Of chaos and happiness.

She was such a bright presence in my bed. Even asleep, she exuded sunshine.

A contrast to my dark storm clouds. The mechanical functioning of putting one foot in front of the other day after day to get through the days. To keep things stable for my pup.

But last night, Joy had needed me. Our interlude had been...unexpected.

Obviously unplanned.

But fate, it had felt good.

It had felt right.

She was an insatiable lover. Passionate. Inventive. Wild. From the first kiss, I felt like I knew her instinctively. What she needed. What got her hot. What got her off.

Everything she wanted, I craved, too.

Her scent covered my skin now. It was on my sheets. It filled the room.

And, like last night when I first picked her up in her mangled bedroom, I had the strong sense that she smelled...*perfect*.

I stared at her, but now a little differently.

Wait...*fuck!*

Was Joy–

Was she *my mate*?

I ran a hand over my beard. Her?

That couldn't be. She was human! And everything I wasn't. We didn't fit together–at all. I couldn't have a fated mate who was so... happy.

In my home pack, no one had heard of a fated mate being human. But almost all the guys at Wolf Ranch, except for Rob, had human mates.

Human *fated* mates.

Not just love matches. But biological mates. The human females had ignited the urge in their wolf mate to mark. Which meant nature intended them to be together.

I was raised to trust my wolf. Trust his instincts. Animals sensed things humans couldn't.

I taught this to Remy as well.

Was my wolf telling me Joy was my true mate? The one female put on this earth for me?

Was that why we were so in sync last night? How I knew her body?

The hairs on my arms stood up with recognition. A lump formed in my throat at the idea of all that brightness belonging to *me*.

To Remy, too.

But that thought made me pull back on the reins.

Fuck. Fate had dealt us a tough blow with Remy's mom being a deadbeat. My little girl's mother had abandoned her. Every time Remy asked after her, I had to explain that it wasn't because there was anything wrong with her. It wasn't that she wasn't perfect and loveable. No one should have those kinds of doubts and especially not a child. Not my Remy.

This thing with Joy could hurt Remy again. Hurt her even more. If I thought an absent mom was painful for Remy, I imagined her confusion and pain if she thought she was getting a new mommy, and then it didn't work out.

Joy wasn't a shifter. She didn't understand what a mate was. How fate supposedly put us together. That I was to mark her and embed my scent in her to make her mine forever.

She knew none of that.

Fate may have picked Joy for me, but there was no guarantee at all that Joy would pick me–*us*–back. Especially because I was a package deal.

The light sound of little feet hitting the floor saved me from doing anything stupid like making this into something, like forever. I quickly stepped out of the bedroom and shut the door.

"Hi, Daddy." Remy emerged from her bedroom with her face slack from sleep and her hair in a massive bird nest.

"Shh." I held my finger to my lips, speaking in a soft tone I knew my daughter's sharp ears would still hear. "Joy is sleeping in there." I pointed at the closed door.

The pleasure on Remy's face seemed to summarize my feelings about having Joy here. Her eyes lit up, and a giant smile bloomed. "She is?" she whispered back. "She had a sleepover?"

I swooped her up in my arms and carried her to the kitchen, so we could make more noise. "Yep. There was a storm last night, and a tree fell on her roof. See?" I held Remy up to the kitchen window to look out. The storm was long gone; the early morning sky was clear and bright. It still was surprising that Remy had slept through the whole thing.

Remy gasped.

A rock rolled over in my stomach, seeing the damage in the light of day. It looked apocalyptic. There was a tree branch in Joy's house, having ripped a hole in the roof and the side wall. I could see framing and sodden insulation.

Joy could have died! If she were a shifter, she'd have been hurt but would have healed quickly. But no. If the tree or any large beams from the house had struck her, I would've lost my fated mate.

The thought made me ice cold. What if I'd found out my fated mate lived next door, only for it to be too late?

No. It wasn't that. I was worried for anyone getting hurt like that. Any neighbor.

"Is she okay?" Remy asked, her little chin wobbling.

I stopped the doomsday thoughts before they got any more traction. Joy was safe in my bed. I'd carried her home and fucked the fear and trauma right out of her. I'd taken care of my mate's safety and needs, not even realizing she was mine.

"Easy, she's fine. You make big messes sometimes, just like that storm."

"Can she keep staying here?"

I shook my head. "She's got her own place. I'm sure someone's going to cover the hole in the roof and the window today, so she can sleep there tonight."

She thought about that for a moment, seemingly appeased because she asked, "Can I go see the storm's mess?"

"*No.*" I answered too sharply–probably infusing alpha command in my voice, which froze Remy's little body.

She might be a wolf with superior healing abilities, but it was still dangerous over there.

Remy was used to my grouchiness, but the alpha command brought out a hurt boo-boo lip. Tears swam in her big brown eyes.

Instant regret washed over me. "I'm sorry, baby. Daddy doesn't want you over there because more of the roof might cave in. That storm's messes are dangerous. I don't want you to get hurt. Ever."

She continued with the hurt puppy eyes, and I gave her a squeeze. "I didn't mean to scare you. Did I?"

She nodded with that lower lip still pushed forward adorably. This kid had me wrapped around every finger and toe.

I set her on the counter to kiss her head.

"What's this?" she brightened, finding Joy's now-cold, untouched cocoa on the counter beside the stove.

"Oh. I made that for Joy, but it's no good now." I took the

mug from her before she could taste it and dumped it in the sink.

"Wait! Daddy!" she cried.

"I'll tell you what. If you eat two eggs and two strips of bacon for breakfast, I will make you hot cocoa. Deal?"

I didn't usually let her have that much sugar or caffeine in the morning, but taking a full mug of cocoa right out of her hand and dumping it was pretty insulting, even if the milk had probably spoiled.

She instantly cheered. "Okay."

I let her stay up on the counter as I reached for a frying pan in the cupboard below.

"Good morning."

My wolf growled with approval when a sleep-tousled Joy stepped into the kitchen, still wearing my flannel shirt–buttoned this time–that hung to her thighs. Fuck, she looked good enough to eat.

"Joy!" Remy hopped off the counter and ran to Joy who gave a surprised little oof as her legs got tackle-hugged.

Now that I knew Joy was my mate, every word she spoke to my kid was significant.

Her quick, easy smile, the brightness in her face, and the way she hugged Remy and tousled her hair meant everything.

I wanted to throw her over my shoulder and carry her back to bed for another round.

My dick stirred at the thought of doing it again.

But no. I needed to push her out the door before Remy got attached.

Hell, I didn't know if Joy even *wanted* another round

with me. She'd been releasing steam last night. Trying to get the adrenaline of the accident out of her system.

Maybe I'd just been a vehicle to an end for that.

It certainly didn't mean she was ready to move in and for me to mark her. To marry me if that was what she needed. It didn't mean she was ready to commit to my kid.

And that mattered. I couldn't let Remy get attached to her and have her heart broken if Joy wasn't interested in us.

I needed to play this right. Joy was human and didn't recognize me as her mate. Johnny, one of the guys who worked at the ranch with me, had told me he'd had to make his new human mate Emma fall in love with him. He'd knocked on her door to kill her boss and discovered she was his fated mate. He'd had to pivot, quickly.

"Making" a human female fall in love was hard enough, but doing it when a four-year-old kid was part of the package was a whole different level.

Especially when I wasn't exactly Romeo. Hell, I was the farthest thing from it. I had the absolute worst track record with females. I'd become the grumpy single dad who didn't know how to plan a date. Hell, shifters didn't *date.*

Looking back, I hadn't been able to satisfy Remy's mom, Soraya, with anything. Fine, I satisfied her with an orgasm the one time we'd fucked on the moon run.

After that, nothing. She'd been needy. Consistently unhappy. She'd bolted the first chance she got. I wasn't enough for her. I had no confidence that I would know how to meet every emotional, physical, and sexual need of my fated mate.

And a human one? With all that fucking sunshine? I'd block it out with all my clouds.

I'd ruin her.

So far, all I'd done was tell Joy how I was going to fuck her and that she was a bad girl for not obeying. Oh yeah, and I'd spanked her gorgeous ass. That might have been hot as fuck, but that wasn't a date. That wasn't forever.

She wanted a night of sex? She got it. Oh, she got it good.

But I didn't have the slightest clue how to make her fall in love.

Nor—far more importantly—*stay*.

But then Joy's gaze met mine, and the warmth of it blasted everything else out.

The sense of rightness settled around me, driving out my objections.

"How do you feel about scrambled eggs and bacon?" I asked, opening the refrigerator to take out the supplies.

She glanced out the window at her house, the pleasant look on her face fading. "I need to make some calls about the damage."

"The house can wait," I said firmly, even though it would probably be better for Remy if I sent Joy scooting out the door. Still, my wolf couldn't stand her not being fed. The need to provide and care for her was too strong. "You need a good meal before you tackle calling your insurance and all that mess."

Remy had her by the hand and led her to the kitchen table.

Still, Joy hesitated.

"Sit down and eat." I sounded grouchy. Formidable. Maybe even intimidating. I needed to work on that. Fuck.

Remy pulled out a chair and patted it. "If you eat two eggs, you get hot cocoa."

To my wolf's relief, my beautiful neighbor sank into the chair. "Your daddy is bossy, isn't he?" Her voice was light, but when I looked over my shoulder, I caught heat and innuendo in her look my way.

Like she *wanted* it bossy.

Wanted me to be the guy who gave it to her hard and told her what to do.

Even liked being my bad girl sometimes.

Fuck, I was in trouble.

11

JOY

TWO HOURS LATER, with a stomach full of eggs and cocoa, I stood in my wrecked bedroom. The wooden floors were swollen and warped from the rain. The rubble was everywhere.

I'd called the insurance company and sent them photos I'd taken with my phone. But I wasn't the only customer in the area who had a storm claim, so they said they'd have an adjuster come out in two or three days. Sooner, if possible.

"Two or three days," I muttered, staring at my flipped bed.

I remembered how Wes had just lifted it and flung it onto its side. I knew firsthand he had solid muscles, but working a ranch sure made him strong.

My inner walls clenched remembering the night before. I was sore, and for a day or two, I wasn't going to forget what we'd done. All because of the storm. Because of the adrenaline.

Because... I'd wanted Wes, and last night there was nothing that was going to stop me from having him. Yup, a storm brought out my inner slut.

It also brought down the ceiling and my roof.

The drywall was broken like eggshells all over everything. Insulation was a fluffy but sodden mound in the middle of the floor. Like sad cotton candy. I looked up into the hole in the ceiling. I could see even more insulation and the framing in the crawl space. I could see past that and outside. Plus, there was the tree limb. It was in the crawl space area and small branches had come through the ceiling and had fallen haphazardly on my bedroom floor.

"I've always wanted a skylight," I said to myself, seeing the blue sky through the hole in the roof. No. That couldn't stay. I had a tarp in the garage I could put over the hole until the repairs could be made.

My cell rang. I grabbed it, hoping it was the insurance adjustor telling me someone could come out today to at least patch the roof.

"Crap." I answered the call because I never knew what my mom's emotional state would be. She often needed me to talk her off some ledge or other, and not always metaphorically speaking. The woman suffered from depression. "Hi, Mom."

"Hi sweetheart."

I could hear the strain of stress in her voice.

Oh boy.

"What's up?"

Something was always going on. Whether it was drama

between her and her sisters or her boss at work or that she'd seen my dad in town, there was always something that triggered my mom.

"Oh, honey, you won't believe what happened. My air conditioner you bought me got damaged during the storm last night."

"Oh no!"

This was Montana. Air conditioners were rare because it didn't get all that hot. Maybe a week of uncomfortable temperatures, but it cooled down at night. But I'd bought my mom a unit a few years ago because her allergies made her so miserable, and she was having trouble sleeping. Depressed people who don't get their sleep could go downhill fast. I knew cool, filtered air definitely helped with allergies and sleep.

"It's terrible! I don't know what to do. Do you think the insurance will cover it because of the storm?"

I sighed, looking at my own insurance nightmare. "Yes, but the deductible probably won't be worth it."

"Oh." She sounded depressed.

Fuck it. I didn't have the money, but I'd figure it out. "Mom, call an HVAC company to come out and take care of it."

"I don't think I can afford it if the insurance won't pay," my mom said weakly.

She worked part-time as a receptionist at an accountant's office. Before my parents divorced, she'd been a stay-at-home mom. Baked cookies, did PTA. Relied on my dad for everything. It was their dynamic. After the divorce, even after all these years, she never really recovered. Never could handle taking care of herself–emotionally or financially.

She cried. She spiraled. She tried–she really did. She'd seem to get her life together, but then something would set her back, and it would all fall apart again.

She couldn't problem-solve for herself–her emotional state just made her shut down when things got complicated or confusing or required any effort.

I've been the one taking care of her ever since my dad divorced her.

She depended on me.

I knew depression didn't make sense. Mom didn't understand that she was supposed to be the grown-up. The parent.

As a teenager, I'd had to be the one whose shoulder she cried on. Who listened to her rant about Dad one minute, then cry about how she still loved him the next. I was the one who paid the bills. Who set a budget. Who got a job at the diner after school to bring in more money, then later at Cody's Saloon, when she'd lose another job because she couldn't get out of bed.

Over the years, nothing had changed. She was still depressed. Still needed me to rescue her.

"Doesn't Clyde offer you more hours?" I asked, referring to her current boss. "You know he's had a crush on you for years. How many times has he asked you out? He'd do anything for you."

"More hours?"

"Yes. More hours–to cover the cost of the air conditioner."

"Your father was supposed to–"

I sighed. Dad again. God. My parents had been embroiled in a years' long custody and child support battle over me, which finally ended when I turned eighteen, and he moved to Missoula.

"Dad left a long time ago. He's never going to pay that child support he owes you. Get Clyde to give you more hours. Or better yet, tell him yes to a date and let him take you out to dinner." I grinned thinking about her out on a date.

She sighed. "I'm too old and–"

"You are not. Clyde wouldn't ask you over and over if he wasn't interested. In *you*."

"Yes. You're probably right. I'll see. No matter what, I just don't think I'll be able to replace it until the first of the month, and it's been *so* hot."

"I know, Mom," I said brightly. "A tree fell on my roof last night, and there's a gaping hole in my ceiling right now."

My mom gasped.

Oops.

This was why I didn't want to tell her. She'd go into full-bore trauma and drama about it when it really wasn't anything I couldn't handle.

"Joy! Sweetheart, are you okay? That's awful! Did you call the fire department? What are you going to do? Oh no. This is horrible."

"It's not horrible, Mom. I figure it's an adventure. It will be like camping in my own house for a while until I can get it repaired. I was just telling myself I always wanted a skylight."

My mom gave another horrified gasp. "Joy, you can't stay there. Sweetheart, it's not safe. And–oh God–you're probably going to get mold!" she wailed. "Was there water damage? Mold can cause all kinds of health problems. Oh, this is a nightmare." In my mind's eye, I could see my mom pacing in her kitchen, wringing her hands over this. "Should I come over and help?"

"No," I said quickly. The last thing I needed was my rain cloud of a mom over here "helping."

"I've got it handled," I reassured. "The insurance will cover the repairs. Don't worry about me. You worry about calling the HVAC guys, okay?"

"Oh. Well, maybe," she said.

She wasn't going to call them or say yes to Clyde. She was just going to suffer and drive me crazy talking about how she couldn't sleep at night without the AC.

Gah. But I didn't have the mental energy to fix this for her right now. I needed to stay positive for myself. I had a damaged pottery order to remake. And I needed to figure out how to at least make my bedroom safe from the elements until the insurance adjusters got here in a few days.

"I gotta run, Mom. Love you!"

"Oh." She sounded disappointed. "Okay, sweetheart. I love you."

I hung up and sighed. It killed me when my mom got depressed, but I didn't have any energy left to rescue her today.

I was too busy rescuing myself.

I was really short on cash this month. I'd anticipated the money for that shipment of pottery that broke. Now, I'd have to spend time remaking it all when the time could have been used on making new things. I had my own house to fix, and that wasn't going to be cheap either.

But on the bright side, my pottery studio in my garage had no damage. I could still throw clay. My business could still run.

I was lucky, truly.

Plus, my living room was undamaged, and my couch was really comfortable. Since there was no way I was staying with my mom–and her too-hot house, I'd be just fine.

I could always get my part-time job at Cody's back. I'd worked there for years when I was getting my business up and running but quit when I was finally making it.

It would be fun. Seeing familiar faces at the bar again. Working late nights.

I needed to get out more, and this was a great way to do it. Right?

12

WES

Having Joy in my house this morning had thrown me off my routine. My brain had been tangled up in how to approach things with her–a problem which I hadn't resolved, especially since my wolf had a very specific opinion–and I'd been late getting Remy to preschool.

Then, when I got to the ranch, I'd discovered I'd left my phone at home.

Not a big deal–I wasn't the kind of guy who spent time scrolling or anything, but once the thought ran through my head that I wouldn't be available if the preschool called, I decided after tackling the usual morning chores in the barn, I'd better run home at lunch to grab it.

I pulled up in front of the house to find–

Oh, hell no.

My mate was standing *on her roof*, a giant blue camping tarp in her hands, about to break her beautiful neck.

What the fuck was she doing?

I leaped out of the truck–only taking enough time to put it into park–and jogged to Joy's house without taking my gaze from her. She had a one story home, but still, the fall had to be at least ten feet.

She was human. Breakable.

She lost her balance, dropping the tarp and pinwheeling her arms to regain it.

"Joy!" I shouted, nearly shifting to wolf form at the present danger.

She found her balance again and simply turned to give me a friendly smile. "Oh, hi, Wes."

My heart was pounding, and my wolf was practically leaping in the air to get to her.

She stood on the roof in a pair of cut-off jean shorts and a triangle-shaped halter top that made me want to lick a line from her bare midriff straight up to one nipple.

I stood beneath her and put my hands on my hips. "Don't you *oh, hi,* me, honey. What in the hell are you doin' up on the roof?" I demanded, forgetting to dial back my aggression, which was fueled by both fear for her safety and lust for her body.

I had no right to talk to her that way.

She didn't need to be scolded.

Yes, she did. She definitely did for being so reckless.

But she was my neighbor, not my girlfriend. My neighbor who I happened to have fucked last night. We weren't committed to each other in any form. I wanted her to be my babysitter.

My wolf thought that was laughable. He was committed to her, but she didn't know that. She didn't owe me anything–including an explanation of why she chose to climb on her crumbling roof.

Apparently, she didn't mind my grouchiness, though, because her smile broadened.

The smile that drove me crazy.

She completely ignored my question. "Can you throw me that tarp I dropped?" She pointed at the lost object.

"Throw you the– Not a chance. What happened to the crew coming to make the repairs?" I asked.

"The adjuster said they'd be by in a few days."

A few days? So she decided to fix it temporarily herself?

"I'll cover your roof," I said, kicking myself for not anticipating her needs before we left this morning. "You need to get down from there before you fall or the rest of the roof caves in."

She mimicked my stance with her hands on her hips and tilted her head to the side. "I can take care of it."

"Not happening," I countered.

"But–"

"No way while I'm living next door are you putting yourself in danger like this."

I should apologize for being an asshole. She probably could put the tarp over the hole on her own. Nail it down. But she could fall and not heal like a shifter. Except she didn't know that was why I was so fucking adamant.

"Oh yeah?" There was a challenge in her voice.

I was fucking this thing up. I opened my mouth in hopes the right words would come out, but then I caught sight of the outline of Joy's nipples.

She wasn't wearing a bra under that barely-there top, and it was clear her nipples had stiffened into points.

At what? The sight of me?

Or was it my bossiness that turned her on?

She'd called me bossy this morning, but the look she'd given me made me think she liked me in charge.

Everything I'd said since I got out of the car was me being bossy and in charge.

Fuck, yeah, honey.

I'll be the boss of you. I'll boss you all the way to my bed.

"Yeah," I countered, then added, "Bad girl," to test it out. To test *her*.

She squatted down to sit on the edge of the roof and kicked her feet like a kid.

She was in flip-flops. Flip flops! On a fucking roof! Cute, but not functional.

"You gonna spank me?" she challenged, cocking her head and giving me that smile again.

My dick got rock hard at her suggestive tone and wondered if her pussy was sore from the pounding I gave her the night before.

Okay. I hadn't misread the situation. Good to know.

I sauntered over until I stood right beneath her. "That's right, beautiful. You have two choices. Climb down that ladder or jump. Either way, if you come down right now, I'll go easy on you." I held out my arms to show her I would catch her.

A flush ran up her neck, and I caught the scent of her arousal on the light breeze.

"You want me to jump?"

"That's right, honey. Jump down, and I'll show you the

consequences of your reckless behavior. It'll be a lesson we'll both enjoy."

My beautiful mate. She didn't hesitate for even a second. She just launched herself off the edge of the roof.

I caught her in my arms, bending my knees and swinging her around to soften any impact she might feel.

"*Damn.*" She sounded impressed.

I liked the way she was looking at me–like I had something she craved. Like *I* was the thing she craved.

"What about my roof?" she asked.

"I'll get to it later. Gotta take care of you first. You're gonna find out what happens when you give me a heart attack like that." I carried her toward my house, flipping her to ride over my shoulder when we got to the door, so I could pull out my keys.

"What?" she shrieked as I tossed her in the air to reposition. "Oh my God. Wes, you are a *beast*."

"Yes, honey, I am." I stepped into the house and carried her to the living room where I tipped her back down to her feet at the side of my couch.

Her cheeks had flushed a pretty shade of pink from being upside down, and they made her blue eyes look bright. Her dimples creased as she looked at me, breath moving faster with excitement.

"God*damn*, you're beautiful." Through her top, I pinched one protruding nipple between the knuckles of my forefinger and middle finger. "I see you pointing at me." Our gazes locked.

Her eyes danced with excitement.

"Turn around, Reckless." I circled my finger in the air. "I'm going to turn your ass red."

She hesitated. "Um, where's Remy?"

"Preschool." I waited, wanting to be sure she truly consented after that answer. That she wanted this. When she slowly turned to face the couch, I filled both my hands with her soft ass and squeezed.

"Good girl," I praised, reaching around to the front of her hips to unbutton her shorts. "Let's get these off you, so I can see my handprints when I spank you."

Her fingers came to mine, so I stopped, again, waiting for consent.

Neither of us moved for a moment. "Take them off," I murmured in her ear then waited for her obedience.

She instantly complied, like the glorious, sweet thing she was. She unbuttoned and unzipped her jean shorts and pushed them down her hips, along with her panties. They hit the floor, and she stepped out of them.

"That's it, honey. Just like that." I caught her wrists and pulled them gently behind her back, then pushed her torso down over the side of the overstuffed sofa arm. It made a perfect bolster for hips.

Holding her wrists pinned to her lower back, I spent a moment admiring her perfect ass–stroking my free hand in a circle around her twin globes. Then I drew it back and gave her a smack.

I went light because she was human, and I would hate to actually hurt her.

When she didn't make a sound, I went harder, slapping the other cheek.

This time she gasped. I stayed at that intensity, spanking one side and then the other for a half-dozen quick spanks.

I was going for a little sting, not anything that would scare her. I stopped to rub, allowing my fingers to slide between her legs.

"You're dripping wet, honey." I dragged my fingers through her nectar and tasted it. "I fucking love the way you taste."

I released her wrists and spun her around to face me. She reached for my belt buckle and undid it.

"You want my cock again, Joy? I thought you might need a break after the way you rode it last night."

She licked her lips as she lowered to her knees. "My mouth doesn't need a break." She unzipped me.

"Oh, damn. *Dayum.*" I wrapped my fingers around her messy bun. "Hell, yes, honey." I helped her by freeing my erection.

She gripped the base and opened her plump lips, then extended her tongue and dragged the head of my cock down it.

A shudder of pleasure ran through me.

"Fuck," I muttered. She made such a beautiful sight kneeling at my feet in nothing but her little halter top, her ass pink with my handprints.

She dragged her tongue around the rim of the head of my cock. The warm heat of her mouth mixed with the cooling effect of the air, creating an exquisite sensation. By the time she took the whole head in her mouth, I was nearly ready to burst.

"Oh, Joy," I groaned. "You're killing me, honey. It's too good."

She lifted her gaze to mine, smiling around my cock before she took me deeper.

This woman was incredible. Not just the blowjob, but the woman giving it. The spontaneous, brilliant ray of sunshine that practically blinded me.

I wanted more of her.

Not just her body, but her heart. Her soul. I wanted her secrets. To find out what made her laugh but, also, what made her cry.

And something about that thought—the idea that I could have it *all* with Joy—suddenly made the idea of *not* having her even more devastating.

I didn't just have to protect my kid's heart in this situation.

I had to protect my own.

I expelled all of those thoughts and instead focused on the pleasure she was offering me. My bold, bright neighbor was taking me as deep as she could. Sucking hard as she pulled back, humming as she went in.

She was *destroying* me.

"Fuck, Joy," I muttered. "Fuck."

She moved her mouth faster over my cock.

I tightened my hold on her bun. "Honey, you're driving me crazy." My breath hitched. "You gotta tell me right now if you want me to come on your face or if you want me to bend you back over that couch and fuck you hard for being such a bad girl."

That got her excited. She pulled off and sat back on her heels, her jaw slack. Her fingers went between her legs to rub. She needed some attention down there.

I reached for her elbows to pull her to stand and turned her toward the sofa.

"Oh, God," she murmured when I pushed her back over.

"You want it deep, honey?"

"Um..."

"You're gettin' it deep. Deep and hard." I pushed her ass cheeks wide and dropped to my knees to taste her sweet pussy. She was dripping wet–even wetter than she'd been after her spanking. Definitely ready to take me.

Still, I took my time tasting her, memorizing her tang, and loving the little moans she made.

I stood up behind her and dragged the head of my cock through her juices, nudging gently at her entrance. She was open and slick, and I slid right in.

"Oh, honey. I can't decide which I love more–your mouth or your gloriously juicy cunt."

She arched her back and took me deeper.

"Mmm, good girl. You want to take every inch of me, don't you?"

She moaned her assent.

"Such a good girl." I slid my fingers around the front of her throat, not squeezing, but holding her loosely there as I rocked in and out of her. I pulled her torso up, so she was arched beautifully.

She loved it. She cried out, releasing even more arousal around my cock.

"Yeah, you wanna come all over my cock again, don't you, honey?" I found a steady rhythm.

"Yes," she moaned.

"You want me to give it to you harder?"

"Yes, please."

I pushed in harder, slapping my thighs into her ass.

She let out a little cry.

"Like that, honey? Or was that too hard?" I did it again.

"It's good," she moaned. "It's so good."

I picked up my speed, plowing into her now. The room filled with the sounds of flesh slapping flesh, her slickness dripping down around my balls. I was getting dizzy with need.

Oh fuck. It wasn't just the need to come. My canine teeth had elongated slightly and were coated with serum. My wolf wanted to mark her.

If I'd had any doubt that she was my mate, it vanished now. One quick bite, and she'd be mine forever.

But, of course, I couldn't do it without her understanding. Without her consent. And arriving at that consent was a problem I didn't quite know how to tackle.

I closed my lips around my teeth and drew in a deep breath through my nostrils, trying to rein in my wolf.

Not yet.

Maybe not ever, I reminded myself. I had to stay vigilant. Keep our hearts–Remy's and mine–out of the game until I was sure it could work.

"Please," Joy begged.

Oh, fuck. My mate was begging? She needed me to give her satisfaction while I was thinking about protecting my heart. What kind of jackass was I?

I reached around to the front of her hips and put the pad of my index finger over her clit.

"Don't come until I tell you," I growled in her ear.

She cried out at the sensation of her most sensitive part being touched. "Wh-what? Why?" she practically wailed. She was desperate to come.

"Because I'm in charge. When I tell you it's time, you're gonna come all over my cock. As hard as you've ever come in your life. Understand?"

She nodded frantically.

I fucked her hard as I tapped her clit with my finger. "Ready…"

My balls drew up tight. I was as desperate to release as Joy. "Set…"

"Please!" she wailed.

13

JOY

I SCREAMED because it felt so good. It wasn't a little tremor of an orgasm, but a body-shaking–no, earth-shaking–kind.

Possibly the neighbor on the other side of my house heard me. My hips jerked, and my internal muscles squeezed and released around Wes' cock, milking out even more of his cum.

He growled, and I felt him fill me, spurt after spurt until it started to slip out down my thighs.

He gave my clit a slow circle, and I came some more– fresh gyrations of my hips and internal muscles. Not a scream this time, but a whimper.

He bucked against me, pressing me harder into the arm of the couch, spilling even more of his essence.

I was wilted and winded, my forehead buried in the soft cushion.

"Don't move, honey. I'll be right back," he said.

My face was turned, so I was able to watch as Wes put his dick away as he went to the bathroom. He returned with a wet washcloth and used it to clean my pussy and inner thighs.

"Fuck," he growled.

He seemed to growl a lot lately although I wasn't sure why this time.

"What?" I asked, pushing myself up.

Wes helped pull me to my feet.

"I've got to get back to work."

"All right."

This guy was hard to read. Was he into me? Just wanted sex? It was hard to know where you stood with a guy of few words who came off as a grumpy bear when he talked.

But I knew he was a good guy.

And not just in bed.

He rescued me last night–and he'd seemed genuinely scared for me when he found me on the roof, not reluctant.

"If I spread that tarp right now, are you going to get back up on that roof?" He pointed in the direction of my house.

I turned, so my back was to him and jutted out my butt. Glancing down at it, I asked him, "I think these handprints are answer enough."

His fingers stroked over one heated spot. "That's right. Go back up there again, and I'll punish the inside of your ass next."

My mind blinked out for a moment. Did he mean–

Holy shit.

"I won't go on the roof."

The corners of his mouth tipped up in a hint of a smile.

I wanted to figure out what it took to get a full grin out of him. "You like that idea. Me putting something in that ass of yours, whether it's a finger or a plug or my dick."

"I do not!" I stammered.

"Yeah, well, you're blushing all the way down to your tits, and your nipples are hard. Your body doesn't lie, honey."

"I... I won't go on the roof."

"Good girl. I'll put the tarp on now before I get back to work. You said the insurance people can't be here for a few days?"

I nodded. "Yeah. They are inundated with claims from the storm. That's why I'm trying to get things covered up now. I don't know how long it will be before they actually start repairs."

Wes frowned and rubbed his beard, his typical grouchy face in full force. "You'll stay here until it's been properly fixed."

Here?

So bossy. It wasn't a question, it was a demand.

I freaking loved it.

After being a mother to my own depressed mom, it was kinda nice to have someone else in charge. Someone taking care of me for a change.

Still, I didn't want to be a burden. "But–"

He cut in, "No way are you sleeping next door with a tarp over the side of your house and another on your roof. That won't keep people out. Or critters."

I opened my mouth to respond then shut it. He had me at *critters,* and he knew it.

"Fine."

I saw the twitch of a smile again. "Are you more afraid of a raccoon breaking in or a bad guy?'

"Definitely raccoon."

His lips quirked higher. It was almost a smile.

I'd take it as a victory.

14

WES

I PICKED Remy up from preschool, and we hit the drive-thru for hamburgers and fries, then the hardware store for plywood.

Even though there was a shit ton of work to do on the ranch, Johnny and Colton were meeting me over at Joy's place to wall up the gaping hole in her window for the time being.

I'd spread the tarp across the hole in her roof, but it wasn't going to be enough to protect the house, even for one night. I needed to build something more stable to keep out the elements and protect her things.

Fate knew how long it would take the insurance to fix her roof if the adjuster wasn't even coming for a couple days.

I now realized I'd been in a protective, sex-induced haze

when I informed her she was staying with me. That had been my wolf talking.

But it went directly against my plan to shield Remy from Joy's radiance. If I didn't want Remy thinking she was getting a mommy, why in the hell did I bring her under my roof?

But I could manage this. Joy was staying while her house was getting fixed, not because I was dating her. As a favor. As a good neighbor. We helped each other. That was the way I needed to present it to Remy.

Not that we were fucking. Or that I wanted to do it again. And again.

"Can I help fix Joy's window with you, Daddy?" Remy asked as I pulled into Joy's driveway.

I unbuckled her car seat and let her climb out of it on her own. "You can supervise," I told her. I learned a long time ago that if you tell a kid what they *can* do instead of what they can't, things went a lot easier.

"You want me to tell you how to do it?" Remy scrunched up her tiny nose.

I booped it with my finger. "You're gonna have to stand back on our porch and let us know if we covered all the holes or not. It's important because we don't want to miss any spots. Okay?"

"Okay." She looked disappointed.

"You can also get beers out of the fridge for the guys. That would be a huge help."

Remy brightened and took off running. "Okay, I'll get the beer!" She made it to the front door and slapped it repeatedly with her palm, as if that would magically open it.

Meanwhile, Joy had come out of her open garage, probably to see why I was parked in her driveway instead of mine.

I took in the sight of the detached building. She didn't use it to park her car. The garage was an art studio. There was a potter's wheel on one side, and a kiln in the back corner. Racks of plain white pottery lined one wall. The other held racks of finished pieces. Beautiful vases, bowls, mugs, and plates in colorful hues were lined up neatly.

"Thank fuck the tree didn't hit the garage," I muttered.

Joy's eyes went wide and a huge smile lit her face. "That's what I said! I figure I got lucky."

I cocked my head trying to figure out that logic. I was a half empty kind of guy, so all I saw was the damage to her house. "I don't know about lucky," I grumbled. "You could've died."

"Daddy! Open the door!" Remy shouted from our house.

"Come and get the key," I told her. She probably wouldn't be able to open the door herself with the key, but I was all about letting a kid try to do grown-up things. It would keep her busy for another few minutes, anyway.

"Oh, I don't know. I'd say I got pretty lucky." The innuendo in Joy's tone got my dick instantly hard.

"Listen...about that and with you staying at our place..." I rubbed the back of my neck.

Remy ran up, and I handed her the key to the front door. "Hi, Joy!" she said. "I'm gonna supervise and get beers!" She raced away, more interested in her job than the neighbor. I was the opposite. I was here for the job, but my attention was all focused on Joy.

"I don't have to stay at your place." Joy waved a hand through the air as if it erased my concern. "I'm definitely cool camping here under my tarp. Even if there are raccoons." She flashed me a smile, and I actually believed her cheerfulness.

Like this girl could make lemonade out of any amount of lemons. Even when believing I had just uninvited her from staying at my house.

"No, no. It's not that." I lowered my voice. "I don't want Remy to know..." I trailed off then swallowed. Fuck it. I needed to be clear with her, so I met her blue gaze head on. "That I'm interested in you. I don't want her to get confused, you know?"

Joy's face softened. "Of course not. I totally understand. I'll just be the neighbor staying on the couch. I mean, if you really are still okay with me being over there."

"I am," I said too quickly. "The clouds are comin' in, and no way are you staying in your place if it's going to storm again."

My wolf needed her under my roof. I wouldn't be able to sleep if I thought she wasn't comfortable or safe.

"So you're...*interested* in me?" Her dimples winked with an impish grin. Fate, she was cute.

I frowned. "I would think that would be obvious."

"Well, I didn't know if it was just about sex. Which is fine if it is." She shrugged. "I mean, I'm the one who jumped you."

Again with the lemonade. It was like she'd learned to keep her expectations of people low so they didn't disappoint. I knew the feeling, but it made me grouchy as hell while it made her sunny.

We had as opposite dispositions as two people could have.

I cleared my throat and took off my cowboy hat to rub my forehead. "Fuck, Joy. I, uh…" Fate, I was bad at this. "To be honest, I haven't dated much–well, at all–since Remy was born." Ever. Just fucked on moon runs, and that was understood in advance that it was nothing. "She took up all my attention. But I'm definitely interested. I just…I also need to be cautious. For Remy."

Fuck. I sounded like a coward.

Was I a coward? *Yes. Because you said you wanted her to be your babysitter.* Dumbass.

She nodded in understanding. "Of course. We can sneak into each other's rooms after dark or something." Joy flashed me that wide grin again.

I felt something foreign launch up my throat. A chuckle. Or the start of one. It made the corners of my mouth tip up. Her smile was almost contagious.

But her suggestion meant she was still only thinking about illicit sex. I needed to make her fall in love. With me. Which would be hard since all I knew how to do was screw her.

"Well, I was thinkin' more like a date, except I don't have a sitter." Everything was so fucking hard with a kid. And a date? Never went on one. What the hell did I know about one? "Maybe her preschool teacher, Riley, could babysit."

"Cody's new wife? She's great."

Johnny's truck pulled up, and he and Colton hopped out. "Hey guys!" Joy waved at them, and I wanted to punch both of their faces in.

When I asked them to help, I hadn't thought about how my wolf would react.

Like a possessive fucker who wanted to poke their eyes out if they even looked at her in those sexy shorts. When they smiled at her, I knew I was going to have to kill them both.

Since I liked them, this was a big fucking problem.

She was already walking out to say hello. "What are you guys doing here?"

I shot forward to get between them. No way were they shaking hands or worse... hugging. "I asked them to come and help me put up a patch on your wall for tonight to keep the rain out. But I don't really need their help." I puffed up my chest and glared at my two friends. "You guys can go back to the ranch."

Colton took off his hat and looked from me to Joy. Maybe it was my fuck-off attitude. Maybe it was the growl in my voice. Maybe he'd been there and understood the feelings I was having right now because he said, "That right?"

"Yeah. Fuck on off." I pointed to their truck. "I got this."

A smile played around his lips. I wanted to punch his smug face in.

Fortunately, Johnny remained quiet. I could take down two shifters at once, especially if my mate was threatened, but even in my obsessed haze I knew it was a bad idea.

"Guys, guys! Here's your beer!" Remy came running out of the house with her arms wrapped around three bottles of beer. I hadn't even realized she'd managed to get in the house by herself. I hadn't been paying much attention to her, and that made me a shit dad.

Of course, one of the bottles slipped out and fell to the sidewalk, breaking. Beer spurted out in a foamy mess.

Remy looked down in shock and then burst into tears.

"Don't move," I barked because she was in bare feet, and there was glass in front of her.

She may have been a shifter pup who could heal swiftly, but I still didn't want her to get hurt in the first place. Especially when it would mean *more* tears.

Of course, my bark turned her crying into a full wail.

I jogged over and scooped her up, but Joy was right beside me.

"Look at all that foam!" Joy exclaimed, like Remy was doing a science experiment instead of melting down over an accident.

Remy stopped crying and gaped at her.

Joy's luscious lips were stretched in a giant smile. She pointed at the foam on the sidewalk with her eyes lit up. "Isn't it amazing?"

Remy wasn't sure if she should buy it.

Joy winked at her. "When I was little, I loved to shake up a can of soda before I opened it to watch it spray. Have you ever done that?"

Remy shook her head slowly.

Joy took the two remaining beer bottles from her hands and set them on the ground before reaching for her. "Come here. I have a can of grape soda at my house. Let's try it."

Just like that, the problem was solved. Remy reached for Joy, who went into her arms and the two of them disappeared into Joy's house. I stood there staring at their backs, and Johnny and Colton stared at me.

"Fuck off," I growled when they walked over.

"How long have you known?" Colton demanded.

"I said, *fuck off*," I snapped.

"Known what? Ohhhhh." Johnny was a little slower to catch on. He jerked his thumb in the direction of Joy's house as I squatted to pick up the glass shards. "She's his mate? I thought he was just being a dick, as usual."

"Definitely his unmarked mate," Colton replied. "Why else would he ask us over to help and then try to kill us when we get within five feet of her?"

"I figured it out this morning," I admitted with a grumble. "Last night, I was too revved up from her almost getting killed by that tree."

Johnny grinned. "Did you guys..."

I stood and took a menacing step in his direction. "I will fucking kill you if you even mention her again."

Johnny laughed and stepped back, his hands up in defense.

"Let's go get that tree off the house," Colton said. "We won't even talk to her."

"Good."

"But *you'd* better," he tossed over his shoulder.

"Seriously. Fuck off." I stomped into my house to dispose of the glass shards and get a broom.

When I got back, Johnny and Colton were on Joy's roof, lifting the felled tree away from the house.

I glanced around quickly. If any human saw them, we were fucked because they were demonstrating way too much strength up there. Then again, there was no easy way to fake lifting a tree off a house, and with their shifter ability, they could do it quickly and easily. We didn't need to wait for the slow-as-fuck repair guys.

"All clear below?" Colton asked me as they held the giant trunk.

"Yeah. Right here." I stood below, so I could redirect it if necessary. The last thing we needed was for the guys to throw the tree trunk off Joy's roof and onto mine.

The guys started swinging it. "On three. Here it comes– one..." –they swung it in my direction, then back– "two... three!" They heaved the trunk off the roof.

I let it fall safely between the two houses, where it broke into a few more manageable pieces.

From Joy's back porch came the high-pitched sound of Remy's shrieked delight and the fizz from an open soda can.

Everything inside me went gooey soft.

Joy was with my pup, just like she had been the day I met her. Easily entertaining her. Making friends. Communing.

Colton and Johnny jumped off the roof without using the ladder. They really should be more careful during daylight.

"She's good with her, huh?" Colton asked, also having heard the girls.

I tried to hide the riot of emotion ping-ponging in my chest. My throat closed. "Yeah. Seems like it."

"Of course, she would be. Fate picked her for you." Johnny slapped me on the shoulder. It made sense he'd understand because Emma, his mate, was an identical twin, and while she and her sister looked exactly the same, even had the same DNA, he knew his mate.

I couldn't say anything. I had arguments in my head about why it might not work and how I didn't know how to make her love me, and what if Remy got hurt, but I didn't want to share any of that with these jackals. I frowned.

"Aw, look," Johnny cackled. "Even having a mate makes Wes grouchy." He quickly dodged back in case I took a swing at him.

Colton's cell rang, and he pulled it from his jeans pocket. "Yeah?" He looked up at the sky. "You got it. We'll be back in thirty."

He hung up. "That was Rob. He wants us back to get the cattle across the creek before it floods again if we get more rain."

Shit. The ranch. My focus had been on my girls, not my job. But Wolf Ranch paid the bills, and Rob was my alpha. If he wanted us to move cattle across a creek, we did.

I ran a hand over the back of my neck. "Shit, he's gotta be pissed we're fucking around in town with all the work to be done."

Colton laughed. "Nah, not when he finds out the reason why."

That I'd found my mate. That she was human.

"C'mon," he said, slapping me on the shoulder. "Let's get that plywood out of the truck and onto the wall."

I stood and watched my friends begrudgingly–one part grateful they were here and had my back and the other half still wanting to murder them for being near Joy. They each had their own fated mate, so they had zero interest in her, but still.

"Daddy! The grape soda had lots of bubbles, too. And it tastes yummy!" Remy ran up to me holding the can.

She had a purple-tinged ring around her mouth.

"I see that," I said.

Joy followed behind at a more sedate pace.

"Think you can wash your face and hands 'cause we're gonna go with Mr. Johnny and Mr. Colton back to the ranch."

I wasn't sure how that was going to work, but I'd figure it out.

I looked to Joy. "The creek flooded last night from the storm. Cattle got stuck on the wrong side. The water's gone down, and we can get 'em across, but it's gonna rain again, and we've got to get to them before–"

Joy held up a hand. "I understand. Your job doesn't have nine to five hours. Why don't I watch Remy for you?"

I stared. Blinked. This was what I'd wanted of her when we first met. Just this. Her being a babysitter. Now? She was volunteering to stay with Remy, and it didn't feel like she was being *just* a sitter.

She was my mate staying with my pup. This was a big deal. I trusted her with Remy, of course, but this was the first time they'd be together alone. Would this make Remy fall for her and then get hurt worse?

Johnny whacked me on the back, breaking me from my thoughts.

"Really?"

She smiled... and my wolf preened.

"Of course. It's no problem. I'm going to work in my studio for a little bit, and she can make a little project. Then we can have dinner and watch a movie."

"Can I? Can I?" Remy pulled on my arm and hopped up and down. "A movie with Joy! Can I, Daddy?"

This was the concern. Joy was too likeable. I didn't have a choice, though. Not only because I had to get to the ranch but because my wolf was telling me to suck it the fuck up and let my mate watch my pup. Because that was exactly what she was supposed to be doing.

Being with Remy in our house. Keeping her safe and loving on her.

"Um, okay. Sure. Let me get your cell number in case you need to reach me. And no going in your house."

She nodded. "No going in my house. Got it."

"Yay!" Remy squealed.

Yeah, it was true.

I had it bad. Because instead of me getting to know Joy, for her to fall for me, Remy was.

I hadn't felt this out of my depth since Soraya left me with a three-week-old pup and zero parenting skills to take care of her.

But I'd figured things out with Remy. Or we'd gotten by.

Maybe I'd find my way with Joy, too?

Fate knew she was worth it.

15

JOY

REMY WAS SO GOOD, it seemed unnatural. She was sweet and listened, had good manners. Did all the things while we were in my studio as I finished two vases and she made a little clay sculpture of her horse. Until she cut her little finger with one of the sculpting tools. She'd cried over the owie. I wrapped a paper towel around it and carried her inside her and Wes' house. I searched for a BandAid in the bathroom and couldn't find any. I checked her small cut, and it was... gone.

So were her tears. Since we were already in the bathroom, I figured it was time to take a bath instead of going back to work on the clay horse. I'd be able to ensure the cut really was gone–or was there one to begin with?–or at least cleaned out. She gave a small temper tantrum, but I lured her in by getting her father's shaving cream–since he had a beard I figured he wouldn't care if it was used–and spreading some on the tile for her to smear and play in. Then, of course, she didn't want to get out.

Finally, after lots of tired-kid coaxing, she was in her pajamas and on the couch. She'd insisted on the movie with the princess she thought looked just like me.

As soon as I settled in beside her, the doorbell rang.

This wasn't my house, so I wasn't sure who to expect. Wes would have walked right in.

"Who could that be?" I asked Remy, who was tucked into my side.

She shrugged but kept her eyes on the screen. Why would she know? She was four.

The rain hadn't started yet, but the evening sky was filled with heavy and dark clouds and the wind had picked up.

I peeked out the side window before I opened the door. Not that a bad guy was going to stand there with a sign that said, *I'm dangerous.*

It was a woman on the porch.

A very pretty woman. Unnaturally so. Raven black hair. Wide set green eyes. Full lips. She was tall. Slim, but had curves. I was very envious.

"Hi, can I help you?"

While I'd given the woman a quick three second assessment, she was looking me over as if judging a cow in the county fair. She took in my sloppy bun, my makeup free face, my old t-shirt, ratty jean cutoffs, bare feet.

Every inch of me was inspected. Then she sniffed.

God, did I smell? It was a warm day, and I'd been in my clay, but I didn't think I was as rank as the way her nose curled up meant.

"I'm looking for Wes." She leaned to the side to look inside past me.

I turned my head and saw Remy on the couch. She was totally engrossed in the movie. "I'm sorry, he's not here right now."

"He's out? And you are?" she asked.

"I'm Joy. Are you a friend of Wes'?"

She laughed, set her hand on her chest. She even had a nice manicure. "A friend? Oh, honey, I'd say we're more than friends."

I frowned. They were together? Was that what she was insinuating?

"Ok-*ay*." I drew the word out.

"He left Remmington alone with you?"

Remington? That was Remy's full name. Cute. But I never once heard Wes use it.

What was her deal? Was she an ex-girlfriend? Jilted lover? I didn't recognize her from Cooper Valley, but she could be new.

"Um, yes."

Remy turned her head at being mentioned. The movie had just ended, so the little girl climbed off the sofa and came to stand beside me. "Hi. Do you know me?" Remy asked with the innocent query of a child.

The woman reached out and tousled Remy's hair, which Remy didn't appear to like because she stepped back and leaned against my leg. "Yes, Remington. I've known you since you were born."

Remy shrugged. "I don't remember."

Maybe I was jealous. If this was an ex or wannabe lover of Wes' I already hated her. She had a bad vibe, and I wanted her out of the doorway. "Well, it's Remy's bedtime, so we need to go."

The woman sniffed again, giving me a cold look. "Tell Wes that Soraya stopped by. He has my number." She looked at Remy. "Good night, Rem-Rem." Her syrupy voice only made Remy lean more into me.

"It's Remy," Remy said from behind my leg.

Soraya turned and walked away.

"That was weird," I muttered, closing and locking the door behind us.

Remy yawned. "I didn't like her." She sounded matter-of-fact. "Even if she is a wolf."

A wolf! So cute, and I loved her childish creative genius. Because the woman *had* seemed like a predator. And had long nails.

"Me, neither," I agreed. "Come on, I see you yawning. I'll read you a bedtime story."

"Okay," Remy agreed and led me to her bedroom. She picked out a mermaid book and climbed under the covers.

I sat beside her on the bed and started reading. Remy's lids grew heavy, and she yawned again. I made my voice soft and soothing. When I finished reading, I didn't move. Remy was already half asleep, snuggled up against me. I quietly closed the book, and she sighed as her little body grew heavier.

Her breathing slowed.

Damn, she was sweet. I leaned over and kissed the top of her head.

Afraid if I moved too soon, she'd wake up, I stayed where I was for another ten minutes and soaked up the sweetness of having a tiny human sleeping against me. It was a preciousness I hadn't experienced before, and it made my chest ache a little.

I'd always wanted kids.

I didn't know where this thing with Wes was going, but I was not at all deterred by the fact that he had a kid and was a package deal. Single dads were not a turn-off for me. If anything, it made Wes all the more attractive. I loved seeing him in daddy mode–the way his gruff exterior softened when he spoke to Remy. The way she was the center of his life.

I knew it meant he'd have less attention available for me, but I didn't care. He'd shown up at my place with his buddies to repair my house, even though they were busy at the ranch. Even though he'd already taken time out of his day to, er... *punish* me.

What a hot punishment that had been.

I heard the sound of his truck pulling into the garage, and my pulse picked up speed. It was as if my body was already conditioned to get excited when he was around.

I carefully extricated myself from Remy to meet him.

Wes walked through the door and took my breath away. He was every inch the muscled, manly rancher, and I found the fact that he did hard physical labor sexy as hell.

I smiled as I walked toward him. "How'd it go?"

He took off his hat and clomped over to me in his cowboy boots. His hands settled on my hips. "Okay. How'd it go here?"

"Great. She's been asleep for about fifteen minutes. But you had a visitor."

His brows lowered. "A visitor?" he asked blankly. "Who?"

I shrugged. "Someone named Soraya."

The color drained from his face. "Soraya. *Fuck*."

"What?" I asked, instantly on alert from the way he spit out the curse. "Who is she?"

He scrubbed a hand over his stubbled jaw, suddenly looking weary. "She's Remy's mom."

16

WES

My blood ran cold.

Joy reached for me. I'd had my hands on her hips before she told me about Soraya, and now she mimicked the gesture, touching my waist, looking up at me with a worried gaze.

She was the only reason I didn't pick up a piece of furniture and hurl it at the wall.

"Fuck," I repeated. My wolf was pacing and snarling, really unhappy that she-wolf came around.

"Her mom? Remy didn't even know her." Shock laced Joy's tone.

I stared into her big blue eyes, one part of me wanting to rampage, the other part soothed by the presence of this female.

Which made sense.

She was my mate.

Unlike Soraya, who'd been nothing more than a quick screw on a full moon run–the shifter equivalent of a drunken one-night stand.

I brought the backs of my fingers to brush across her cheek, wanting to soak in the well-being that emanated from her. Or that she produced in me.

It was as if being near her was somehow healing.

The simmering rage I'd had in me ever since the day Soraya abandoned her pup at only a few weeks old was calmed by this gentle female's touch. By her compassion.

I wasn't the type to talk about myself. I kept things bottled up. Didn't share much with anyone, but Joy was my mate. She deserved the truth about my past. "She walked out just weeks after Remy was born. She couldn't hack being a mom."

"Oh, shit." Joy stared up at me. "Poor Remy. Poor you. That's awful."

"It was the worst. Not because she broke my heart, hell no, but because she gave up." I ran a hand down my face, knowing I was sweaty and grimy from moving a shit ton of cattle. My rough time at work was nothing compared to those early months with Remy. "I didn't know a goddamn thing about tending a newborn. I was a rodeo rider. I'd stupidly thought my job would be to provide for Soraya and the pup."

"The pup?" Joy's lips quirked up as she gave me a quizzical look.

Shit. *Shit.* "I mean baby. Did I say pup?" I shook my head. "Fuck, it's been a long day."

"It has." She took my hand and led me to the couch.

She threw me for another full loop when she tugged my cowboy boots off.

It was somehow more intimate than the sex we'd had. More intimate than the hot spanking I gave her this afternoon. More intimate than anything we'd already done. It was simple. Quiet. I liked the idea of coming home to her. To her taking care of me. It was sexy and kind at the same time.

It was something a real partner might do. Someone you'd been with for years and had a level of comfort and mutual care with.

I blinked hard at the sudden rush of emotion that hit me–a mixture of longing and gratitude.

All I could do was stare at her with hunger and admiration. Desire and the need for deep connection. I took a deep breath, reveled in her familiar scent. I'd know it–and her–anywhere now.

I reached for her waist and tugged her onto my lap. "That was so fucking sweet," I growled into her neck, so she wouldn't see how much it had meant to me.

She wrapped her arms around my neck and ran her fingers through my hair, fluffing it where my hat had flattened it.

"Careful, honey, I'm pretty rank," I warned.

She laughed. "The way Soraya sniffed me, I smell pretty bad, too."

I stilled. Fuck. She knew Joy was human. Did that matter? I had no idea why she'd dropped by, but I had a feeling I'd find out. Her visit wasn't a one time thing. She was coming back, I was sure of it.

"So she hasn't been a part of Remy's life?" Joy asked. "You have full custody?"

"Custody...shit. I don't have any paperwork. I mean, she left, and I did my best."

"And she never came back?"

Here was the dark truth. One Joy might judge me for. Humans believed in things like shared custody and shit like that.

"I, uh, I quit the circuit, but I'd heard she'd moved back to our hometown, so I took the job here at Wolf Ranch instead."

"I don't blame you for setting boundaries like that," Joy said immediately. "I mean, the last thing you'd want is Remy getting attached to her and having her ghost Remy again. A newborn's one thing; they don't remember. But a four-year-old won't forget."

Relief swept through me. "Exactly. I'm so glad you understand."

"So she hadn't seen Remy since she left?"

I shook my head. "No. Like I said, we traveled from one rodeo event to the next. We came through Montana and Boyd Wolf–an old buddy from the circuit–came to see us. When he saw I was raising a kid on the road like that, he offered me a job on Wolf Ranch. At that time, I was grateful for the opportunity to steer clear of our hometown and her. Also, I'd hoped being here meant she couldn't easily find me. Us. She walked away. She made her choice."

"What does she want, do you think?" Joy asked.

My jaw clenched, and I tightened my hold on her. I wanted to rip off my clothes, shift, and run–track down Soraya and get her to talk. But I wasn't leaving my girls alone. Not now. No fucking way. "Remy, of course. She's here for Remy. The question is why?"

"Could she be back for you?" From the way Joy tensed as she asked the question, I realized I should have made that part clear from the start.

"We were never together. There was no love involved. We weren't a couple." I tried to say it as many ways as I could so she would understand there was no competition. "It was a one-night thing before I went back to the rodeo circuit. I didn't even know she was pregnant until I came back to town six months later. She never told me. Hell, we didn't exchange numbers. When I found out, I tried to do the right thing by renting a decent house and moving her in with me. I bought all the baby supplies, childproofed and everything. Then she bailed as soon as she could." I cupped the side of Joy's face. "We weren't a couple. Never, honey. I've only known you for two days, and I feel more for you than I ever felt for that she–" I stopped myself from saying *she-wolf*.

"–devil."

Joy raised her brows in laughter. "She-devil?"

I shrugged. "I didn't want to call her a bitch in front of you."

She laughed and some more of the rage Soraya's unexpected visit brought on left me.

"I like your laugh."

She quieted, but her wide smile lingered as she touched my lips. "I want to hear yours."

The corners of my lips quirked. "It might break my face," I said, repeating the taunts the guys at the ranch always threw my way. They repeatedly said I had "resting bitch face."

She laughed again. "I'm willing to risk that."

Damn. She pulled an actual smile from me. And it didn't even hurt.

No, it felt good. Weird, but good.

She lowered her face and kissed my lips. I lifted her waist to adjust her legs to straddle my lap, facing me, and kissed her back.

"Joy, I do want to get to know you. I want to date you. Meet your family. *And* fuck you six ways until Sunday."

She grinned and untied her halter top at the neck, so it fell down.

My wolf roared to life so fast at the sight of her perfect tits, I was afraid my eyes were glowing.

"How about we get started on that part tonight?" she asked in a husky voice.

I yanked her hips over mine, my dick already thick. "I'm your man."

17

WES

"What do you think we'll find today?" I asked Johnny and Boyd as I adjusted the blanket on the back of Sunshine.

Sunshine. It made me think of Joy. I still had her taste on my tongue from an early morning tryst before Remy woke.

We were in the stable at Wolf Ranch saddling up our horses. The morning chores had been done, and it was time to ride the west side of the property to check for storm damage. Sections of the creek washed out some fencing on the east side–and stranded a bunch of cows, so we expected something similar in the other direction. "Downed trees?"

"Hey, Johnny. You think Wes looks like he's smiling?" Boyd asked, lifting his saddle from the rack.

I could feel Johnny eyeing me. "I think you're right. Maybe finding his mate was the cure for his cantankerous nature."

"We've been looking for that stick up his ass. Maybe he just needed to get laid."

"Watch it," I growled although I couldn't help the way my mouth tipped up.

"That *is* a smile," Johnny added, pointing and grinning too.

Boyd came over. Slapped me on the shoulder. "Good for you, friend."

"Good for Wes, what?" Rob came into the barn.

"He found his mate. Next door neighbor."

"Sounds a little like you, brother," Boyd told Rob. Rob's mate was Willow, who from what I'd heard, used to live on the ranch that shared his fence line.

As alpha, Rob was quieter than Boyd. Calmer. He didn't talk as much either. But when he did speak, everyone listened. And it wasn't because he used alpha command either. He'd been made alpha for a reason.

"That right?" Rob tucked his thumbs in his jeans pockets.

"Yeah. Joy Wallace."

"She does ceramics, right?" Rob asked.

I nodded.

"Someone got us one of her vases as a wedding present. It's on the sideboard in the dining room."

"We were commenting on how he's smiling," Boyd said.

"Marked her then. Congrats." Now *Rob* smiled.

I shook my head as I patted Sunshine's soft nose. "Not yet. I just met her two days ago when I moved in. A human fated mate is tricky."

All three of them laughed in agreement.

"Hell, you don't think we know?" Boyd asked. "I had to

minimize how quickly I healed after being gored by a bull with Audrey."

"I had to tell Emma not only that I'm a shifter, but an enforcer, too. Fun times," Johnny added.

Rob grumbled. "Well, lock that down soon." Meaning get Joy to fall for me, agree to be mine, be okay with me *and* Remy being shifters, wanting me to bite and mark her, and, oh yeah, fall for us.

"I can't rush things," I told him. "I've got Remy to think about."

Rob leaned up against the stable wall. "What's your concern? Joy doesn't like kids?"

My throat grew tight remembering how sweet she was with Remy. "No, she and Remy get along great. But what if it doesn't work out? I don't want Remy hurt."

Rob gave me a hard stare. "If it doesn't work out, a four-year-old's feelings are the least of your concerns."

I bristled. "How so?" I asked.

He cocked his brows. "Moon madness."

Moon madness. Shit. I hadn't even thought of that. It must be because I was getting on in age, which made me more susceptible. While I wasn't alpha of my pack, I was alpha through and through–another marker for the insanity that came on if a wolf didn't mark his fated mate.

"Add to that, you tell her you're a shifter, and she bails instead of getting marked, we've all got a problem," Rob said.

I ran a hand over the back of my neck. "Shit, I'm just worried about Joy not liking *me* enough to stick. I don't want Remy to get attached and then upset when Joy walks.

Her mother did that to her, but at least she doesn't remember."

My jaw tightened at the thought of Soraya showing up unannounced last night. I needed to figure out what the hell she was up to.

"If she's still around after your grumpy attitude the other day, there's hope." Johnny tightened the flank cinch on his saddle.

"I know. I need her to fall for me. For me *and* Remy. Because Remy comes first. If Joy's not the one, then maybe my wolf is wrong about her being my mate."

"Or you'll go moon mad, and we'll have to put you down," Rob added.

Colton shook his head. "Shit, now who's the grumpy one? Can't you be happy for the guy?"

Rob shrugged. "I'm alpha. I have to think of the pack. Let me know if there's anything we can do to help."

"Actually..." I began.

I didn't like to ask for help. I had a lone wolf personality, but the Wolf Ranch pack was teaching me more about trust.

The three men stared at me.

"Remy's mom showed up. Came to the house last night when we were moving the cattle."

"She wants you back?" Colton asked.

"I don't know what she wants. Soraya's... well, she's a bitch, and she left her kid."

They'd already heard my story, but they shook their heads at the idea of a mother abandoning her own pup.

I shrugged. "She sure as hell isn't here for me. One full

moon fuck wasn't a draw for her. There's no way she's back for more, especially after four years."

"She's here for Remy," Rob surmised.

I nodded. "That's my guess. But why now?"

Rob looked to Johnny and tipped his chin. "Get on it. Find out anything you can about her, so we can figure out her angle. I'll take your horse while you get started."

Johnny was our pack's new enforcer. When Rob offered to help in any way, I imagined babysitting or something. But this? I sighed because it felt good to have a pack at my back. I wasn't alone in this.

Johnny nodded. "You got it, Alpha." He looked to me, gave me a reassuring smile, then cut out of the stable.

"Might take a little bit, but he'll find out what she's up to," Rob assured me. "If someone in my pack is being threatened, even from a she-wolf, I want to know."

I tipped my head. "Thank you."

He eyed me. "Your job is still to get your human to fall for you. The alternatives aren't all that great."

Like Colton said, now who was the grumpy one?

18

JOY

It was after dark when I stepped beneath the hot spray with a long sigh. I would go over to Wes' after I took a shower and felt more like myself.

I tipped my chin down, closed my eyes, and let the one splurge I made when I bought my house–the fancy shower head–beat hot water against my back in just the right way. I'd just come home from my mom's house, and I was fighting the sensation of defeat.

I wasn't the kind of person to say I'd had a shitty day, but...if I were, this was one. Definitely.

I groaned aloud, the sound bouncing off the avocado green tiles.

No, I should be grateful. I'd started the day with Wes' head between my legs, and I'd probably end it that way, too. To say he was talented with his tongue was an understatement. Maybe I was insatiable. Maybe he was just that good, but I came fast. Record speed.

I had zero reasons to complain.

Things could be much worse. I could suffer from depression like my mom.

She'd been in a funk today, which was why I'd gone over. She hadn't been able to get a new air conditioner which meant she wasn't sleeping, which meant she couldn't keep herself together. She'd considered telling Clyde yes to a date, but that made her anxious. What if he changed his mind and turned her down? All the usual girl thoughts circled her brain.

She'd called in sick to work today because she couldn't get out of bed. When I saw her, she was in a very dark place. I never knew when it was bad enough that I should take her to a hospital or something.

She'd never tried to self-harm, so at least I didn't have to worry about that.

Still, she was my mom, and I wanted her to be happy. It was hard to watch someone not even try.

To add to my gloominess, the insurance adjuster showed up to inspect the damage, and it sounded like it was going to be weeks before I even found out how much they would pay for the renovations. I could hire someone to do the work sooner, and I'd be reimbursed, but I couldn't afford it.

I needed to follow up on my idea of picking up some shifts at Cody's for extra cash. That meant all day in my studio and late nights slinging drinks.

I sighed again because I was tired just thinking about it.

Bright side. Think of the bright side. My business was

going great, and the setbacks weren't something a client saw. I made pottery. It broke. It could be so much worse. I was lucky enough to know Cody and have been a previous employee. It'd be easy for me to transition back. I was lucky to be able to get a fill-in job like that one in such a small town.

I was lucky.

Right?

I stepped out of the shower, wrapped a towel around myself, and then headed to my bedroom to find some clothes. It was still a disaster inside. The bed pushed up on end, mostly blocking my closet. I hadn't even been in with a broom to clear the rubble because I wasn't sure if the roof would collapse on me if I did. There was no light since the ceiling had collapsed and took the sconce with it, so I had to rely on the hallway one to try to see.

"Joy?" The sound of Wes' deep voice calling from my back door didn't startle me. It sent a surge of pleasure and comfort through me. Like Wes belonged in my house. In my life.

"I'm in the bedroom," I called back.

"You'd better not be."

I smiled at his bossy growl.

"Well, my clothes are in here. I can't very well run around naked, can I?"

His heavy footsteps announced his approach. "It's not safe." In a matter of seconds, he was in the bedroom, picking me up by the waist, and swinging me around to put me back in the hallway. My towel dislodged and dropped in the doorway.

"Fuck, honey." His eyes seemed to glow bright green as

he glowered at me. His gaze dipped to my breasts, and he growled in a low animalistic rumble. "Definitely nothing wrong with naked," he muttered, stooping to pick up my towel as he took a slow perusal of my body.

I chuckled and felt my nipples harden.

Slowly, taking way more time than was needed, he wrapped the towel back around me, looking his fill first. "*I'll* get your clothes out of there. Fuck, I'm sorry I didn't think to do it yesterday. But why are you even over here? Not only am I not sure about your roof caving in, but you have broken electrical wires hangin' in here. You could be electrocuted."

Some of that sense of defeat started to creep back in. He wasn't helping me keep my thoughts positive.

My house was a literal disaster, and I had to live like this for weeks if not months.

"Why didn't you shower at my place?" he demanded.

My shoulders sagged. "I...had a rough day. I just needed to be alone for a little bit to get myself together before I came over."

"Together?" Wes' lifted me straight up before I knew what was happening with his forearm beneath my ass. He pinned me against the wall of the hallway and pressed his body against mine, bringing us nose to nose, my feet hovering a foot above the ground. I could feel his hard dick through his jeans, and he had it pressing right against my pussy. I whimpered, then rolled my hips. "What does that mean?"

I sighed. "It means I didn't want to bother you or Remy with my crankiness or my bad day."

He huffed out a laugh. "You? Cranky? I think I'm the

one who's always cranky. Honey, you don't have to get your-self together for me. You don't have to hide your bad day. Not for Remy, either. She's four. I know you've seen her fuss and have a tantrum. And me, well, I guess I have a grown-up version all the time."

My eyes smarted. Ack. I didn't want to cry, even though what he said was funny. And true.

I tried to kiss him, to divert the rush of emotion, but he remained still, not kissing me back.

I drew back, perplexed.

"I'll fuck your brains out, if that's what you need, Joy, but maybe what you really need is a good cry. If that's true, I'd rather hold you and listen."

A sob rocketed up my throat. I didn't *want* to cry. Even standing in the middle of the disaster that was my house, the perfect place to let my feelings drown me.

"Put me down," I choked.

Wes' brows were down low. He eased me back to my feet but didn't let me go. I gave a playful shove at his chest to move him–I sure as hell didn't want to stand here feeling so exposed while he stared me down–but he didn't budge.

God, I felt more exposed emotionally than when the towel dropped a minute ago and left me bare.

"Wes," I breathed.

"It seems to me," he said slowly, studying me, "that you're the type of person who is very good at lifting others. You're cheerful and kind. You're the sunshine in the middle of a storm."

I blinked hard, but the tears were starting to fall.

"I love that about you," he admitted.

He loved that about me.

"But it's also okay for you to not be okay."

I leaned my forehead against his broad, muscled chest, starting to cry for real now. His arms banded around me.

"You don't always have to make lemonade out of lemons. Sometimes, things just suck. Or break, like your damned roof. We can hunker down in the covers together with our arms around each other and just be with each other through the pain. As long as it's in my bed, not yours."

Oh my God.

I lost it completely.

I sobbed into Wes' chest, not even sure where all the emotion was coming from. Probably from half a lifetime of being cheery to my mom's depression, I supposed.

What would happen if Mom saw me cry? Would she sink even further into one of her funks? I always had to show her what it looked like to be happy.

Wes didn't move, only stroking his big hand up and down my back. He was my rock, holding me as I allowed it all to come out.

Then, because it felt so out of control to cry and yet also so good, I started to giggle through my tears.

Wes pulled my face away from his now dampened shirt and gazed down with concern. "Are you laughing?"

"Yes. No. I think so," I laugh-cried. "The crying feels good, so I'm laughing." I laughed harder, tears streaming down my cheeks.

A puff of laughter came out of his lips.

"You laughed!" I accused, pointing my finger at his face. His smile made me laugh so hard my stomach cramped. I doubled over, slapping his chest.

He chuckled.

I laughed harder.

Then, suddenly, we were on the floor of my hallway, with me cradled on Wes' lap, leaning into one of his strong arms. I wiped my tears, alternating between laughing and crying.

Wes alternated between chuckles and kissing the top of my head.

Finally, exhausted, I leaned back in his arms and sighed.

He stroked my arm. "What happened today, honey?"

"It was nothing, really. Just that I won't get the insurance money to fix the house for at least another month or so, and... my mom."

"She okay?"

"Yes. I mean, physically, yes. Mentally, she's having a rough time. She's suffered from depression ever since my parents divorced."

Wes grunted. "Was it messy?"

I nodded. "It was messy. There was a custody battle that went on for years and years. It was probably more about my dad not wanting to pay child support than that he really wanted me to live with him. My mom just never could function under all the stress of it."

Wes kissed my bare shoulder. "And you took on the job of lifting her."

I went still. Had I? "Yeah." I twisted my neck to look at him. "You're right, I guess I did."

"It makes sense, psychologically. She was your mom–the figure you depended on to survive, as a child. Of course, her mental well-being was utmost to your own survival. You became Ms. Sunshine."

That made me tear up again, compassion for my younger self seeping in. "Yeah, Miss. Toxic Positivity."

"Not toxic," Wes assured me. "But maybe you avoid the unpleasant emotions because they scare you."

I blinked rapidly. "Yeah." Memories of my mom getting upset if I was sick or sad flashed through my mind. "I didn't want to make her sad. And I especially didn't want to end up like her."

"So she's not doing well now?"

"Today? No. She isn't sleeping well, which exacerbates her depression. I brought dinner over and tried to cheer her up, but..." I sighed.

"How can I help?"

"Got an extra air conditioner lying around?" I joked.

"Actually, yes."

My head popped up. "You do?" I asked, stunned.

He grinned. Actually grinned. It transformed his entire face and made my chest warm. "Yeah. It's at the ranch. I guess there was a hot spell last summer, and Johnny bought a window unit for his room in the bunkhouse."

"He's not using it?"

Wes shook his head. "Nah. Rob had A/C installed. I'll bring it home tomorrow, and we can take it to your mom's. I'll put it in for you. How's that sound?"

"That sounds amazing. Thank you so much."

"Good." He lifted me off his lap and stood. "Right now, I'm going to move your clothes out of the bedroom, and you're gonna get your sweet ass over to my place. And tonight, after Remy's in bed, you've got a punishment coming for putting yourself in danger again." Wes' face took on a wolfish expression.

My pussy clenched. Nipples tightened.

"Oh yeah? What kind of punishment?" I put a purr into my voice.

"The kind where you end up with a red ass and a dripping wet cunt." Wes' voice was rough and raspy. It went straight to my lady bits.

My clit pulsed in a slow, steady thrum. I loved him bossy. I loved him grumpy. I loved him heroic and showing up for me in a way no one had before.

It seemed crazy and too soon, but I was falling for this guy. Hard.

He squeezed my ass with a rough, possessive grip, then kissed me like he meant it.

"I can't wait," I breathed when he broke the kiss.

His eyes seemed to glow green in the darkness. "Fuck. Me, neither."

19

WES

THE NEXT NIGHT AFTER WORK, Remy, Joy, and I brought the air conditioner over to Joy's mom's place.

With advanced notice, Mrs. Wallace was waiting at the front door for us when we pulled up. If Joy hadn't told me she'd been in a funk, I wouldn't have known. She and Joy looked so much alike with their fair hair and blue eyes. While Mrs. Wallace's weren't as alive as her daughter's, they certainly brightened at the sight of Remy.

I'd have to give Remy extra marshmallows in her hot cocoa because she took to *Miz Wall* right away, yakking her ear off about her day at preschool, then pretty much conning the older woman into making cookies.

All I'd done was shake her hand when Joy introduced me, then installed the window unit in her bedroom.

Seeing how happy–yes, happy–all three of them were, I decided to let them have some girl time and headed home.

Thank fuck I had.

Not ten minutes after I got back, Soraya showed up. I wasn't sure if her timing was intentional or not.

"I'm here for Remington," she said after I opened the door then leaned against the jamb. I wasn't letting her in, and the action made that very clear.

"She goes by *Remy*, which you'd know if you'd been around."

Soraya cocked a hip, allowing her shoulders to sink in defeat. "I want to be a mom to her."

I hadn't seen Soraya in all this time. She looked the same. She looked good even. Sleek dark hair. Pale skin. Tall and slim. But I knew her heart. I knew her nature, and it was ugly.

"Yeah, then I guess you shouldn't have left four years ago," I countered.

"I know I shouldn't have left. I just got scared. I didn't know anything about raising a pup, and she was so tiny and helpless."

Fate, I remembered those long nights holding a crying infant who wouldn't sleep. Cursing Soraya for leaving us.

"I didn't know anything about it, either," I countered. "But I didn't bail on the tiny pup whose life depended on me."

"Yeah, I knew you'd be better at it. I figured I'd fuck her up. I was a mess. But I've got myself together now, and I want her back. She's my daughter."

"What's the female version of a sperm donor? Surrogate? You were just a womb for her to grow. Nothing more."

Harsh? Hell, yeah.

I watched as her face hardened. Whatever she was

playing at before–being sorrowful or honest–was just that. A game.

"What do you really want, Soraya?"

"I want Remy." She crossed her arms over her chest. The contrast between Soraya and Joy was blatant. Soraya exuded... greed. She wanted Remy for some reason and expected to get her. I thought of what Joy had said about her dad fighting for custody to avoid paying child support. Could she want Remy, so I'd have to pay her support?

Except she was delusional if she thought I'd ever give up my kid. I had a heart. Unlike her.

She'd stopped by as if she were asking for a cup of sugar, and I'd hand it off, and she'd leave. 'Cause you didn't return sugar.

Joy was a giver. She gave and gave until she was empty. I knew what she was like when that happened. It would be my job as her mate to refill her as she needed it because her brightness replenished me.

Soraya on the other hand? She was a leech.

"Not happening."

She arched a brow. "Really? You don't have a say."

"I don't? Are you insane? She's been mine since the second you told me she was too much, that you needed out. She's my child. My fucking life. I have *all* the say."

She didn't cower. Not even the slightest. "When the council hears you're shacking up with a human, they'll give her to me."

I suddenly went cold. Very, very cold. I also wanted to reach out and throttle her, but that wouldn't kill her. She was threatening me with Joy.

"I can smell her on you." Her nose crinkled up as if the scent was foul.

I loved having Joy's scent all over me. My wolf was soothed by it.

I tipped my chin up. "Get gone, Soraya. Go back from whatever hole you crawled out of. Leave us the fuck alone."

She took a step toward me. Tipped her chin back so our eyes held. "I'm calling a council hearing, and they're going to side with me."

"Yeah, good luck with that," I growled although I wasn't too sure.

Would the council side with her? Did they make choices in favor of she-wolves based on their biology? Did they try to prevent a pup from being raised in a mixed family?

"I'll be back." Soraya headed down the walk with a toss of her long, thick hair.

I watched until she was in her car and down the street. Then I pulled out my cell and called Johnny.

"Got any info yet?" I asked.

Johnny laughed. "Hello, to you, too. Back to your grumpy self, it seems. Shouldn't your mate be–"

I cut him off. "Soraya stopped by again. She's here for Remy."

"Shit, man. Sorry. Let me check my email from my contact in your old pack."

I went inside, shut the front door, then paced. Thank fuck the girls weren't here. I'd scare both of them right now. Thank fuck it was a full moon tomorrow, and we could run.

"Nothing yet."

I sighed, rubbed my forehead. "Shit."

"If there's something there, we'll find it," he vowed.

"There's something there. That woman's like Jekyl and Hyde. She's trying her hardest to be sweet, so I'll just give in, but when I fight her on it, her she-claws come out."

"She sounds fun," Johnny muttered.

"She mentioned taking it up with the council."

"Haven't heard anything yet," he said. "I'd know because you're in my pack, and I protect you."

Johnny was a kid in comparison to me, and he had the job of protecting me. I appreciated it and him.

"Let me know if you hear anything."

"Will do."

Now I had to wait. Tried to be like Joy and feel all sunshiney, but I knew after trying for two seconds that wasn't going to work.

My ex was after Remy. I wouldn't be happy until this was fucking resolved.

20

JOY

I DIDN'T REMEMBER a time when Mom seemed so... bright.

Little Remy worked her four-year-old wiles on her and got cookies. Hot cocoa. A princess movie. A special movie blanket–which was an old pink one Mom found in the closet. Even apple juice with two maraschino cherries added.

To say Remy had been spoiled was an understatement.

To say I didn't care because Mom was loving every moment of it was also an understatement.

Mom smiled.

Mom laughed.

Mom cuddled.

Mom was the mom I remembered from when I was little.

Did I think she was cured of her depression? Hell, no.

But it was a good day, and hopefully, she and Remy could spend time together again.

When Wes picked us up, he had to carry Remy to the car because she was sound asleep. She didn't wake when he tucked her in bed when we got home either.

"What's the matter?" I asked after he closed her bedroom door. I knew the silence in the car wasn't because he didn't want to wake his daughter. If she slept through a storm and a tree falling through my house, she could sleep through our voices.

No, something was wrong. I was used to his grumpy nature, but he radiated anger and frustration. I wrapped my arms around him.

"Tell me," I said against his shirt.

"Soraya came back."

I pulled back, looked up at him.

"What happened?"

"She said she wants Remy. I told her to get lost."

"Did she say why?"

He ground his molars together and shook his head.

I took his hands. "What are we going to do?"

I knew nothing about child custody laws, but I knew how good of a father he was. If Soraya abandoned her own daughter right after birth, then there had to be some precedent that Wes would keep custody. Still, it was scary, and Remy wasn't even my child.

I was invested in this. I ached for Wes and felt fierce for Remy because that woman didn't have a motherly bone in her body.

The corner of his mouth tipped up. "I like the way you said 'we.'"

I climbed into his lap, cupped his face. "You helped me, now I'm helping you."

Somehow.

"We have to wait to see what happens next. Respond accordingly."

That was a horribly vague answer, but really, there wasn't much to do until we had something to react and respond to.

Until then, we had to wait. I had to soothe Wes, somehow. Words might work a little, but I knew what would calm him because when I'd been frazzled from the tree falling through my house, he knew what would calm me.

I kissed him. Fiercely.

He kissed me back, taking over. Yes, he needed this. I'd give it to him.

I rolled my hips against him, and my pussy lined up perfectly with the rough denim of his jeans.

"Wes," I whispered.

"Mine," he growled. Then he gripped my hips and stood.

I wrapped my legs around his waist as he carried me to his bedroom. We'd figure out what to do about Soraya. Together.

21

JOY

The next evening, I was settled once again on the back lawn of Rob and Willow Wolf's sprawling ranch house. Marina had invited me over to hang out with the women of Wolf Ranch tonight while the men moved more cattle.

Since my house was borderline condemned, at least temporarily, and there was a chance for crazy-Soraya to stop by again, I was thrilled to spend the evening away from Wes' house.

Remy was inside watching a movie with Lily, the daughter of Clint, another rancher.

Having lived in Cooper Valley my whole life, I knew most of the women here, but it was a delight to get to know them better. We sipped wine and nibbled on a gorgeous array of charcuterie. It seemed Marina did more than bake. I loved to be included as one of their group. There was a close knit feeling here at the ranch–not just among the men, but among the women, too. Luckily for me, it seemed that the moment I started dating Wes, they included me as part of their posse.

I was honored.

The group included Marina, who I loved, and her sister Audrey, Boyd Wolf's wife and a local OB/GYN. Then there was Becky, who worked as a nurse with Audrey. The toddler, Lily, was hers.

Riley, Cody's wife was here, and Emma, a newcomer from Los Angeles, who was dating Johnny. Natalie owned the ranch next door to Wolf Ranch, and last around the circle of chairs was Charlie, the ranch veterinarian.

"Where is Willow?" I asked, referring to Rob Wolf's wife.

"Oh, she's helping the men, actually," Marina laughed.

"Good for her." I popped an olive in my mouth. Willow seemed like a badass. If I understood correctly, she'd been undercover on Natalie's ranch with the FBI when she met Rob. Insane!

Just then, Lily came running out, the screen door slapping behind her. "Mommy, I want to run with the wolves, too!"

A couple of the women glanced my way and laughed as Becky scooped the child up onto her lap for a cuddle.

"Are we the *Women Who Run with the Wolves*?" I remembered the book my mom had by her nightstand years ago.

Marina laughed lightly. "Well, it *is* Wolf Ranch, so we have to make all the wolf connections we can."

"Right," I agreed and stood. "Let me go check on Remy," I said, since she would be alone in the house now. She'd been to the ranch more than me since she spent time here while Wes worked, but the house was big, and I knew she was a little afraid of the bad queen in the movie.

"She went to run with the wolves," Lily said, tucked into her mom's chest.

"Oh, she did?" I asked brightly. "Well, maybe I will go, too." I went inside to the living room where the girls had been watching a movie, but Remy wasn't there.

Where was she?

I looked in the bathroom and the kitchen but didn't see her. "Remy?" I called.

A niggle of misgiving ran through me.

"Remy?" I shouted.

Now I understood why Wes had been so grumpy the evening we first met. He'd been worried when he couldn't find his girl. Of course, he had. But now that I was dealing with the same thing, I had to fight a rising panic.

I swiftly walked back out to the lawn. "Lily, where did you say Remy went?"

Lily pointed away from the house. "Outside. To run with the wolves."

Outside. Okay.

There was probably nothing to worry about. The ranch was safe. Remy was probably just out on the front porch.

I hoped. Still, my pulse raced as I reversed directions and jogged back through the house–just in case she'd been hiding inside–to the front door.

"Remy?" I threw open the screen and stepped outside.

Remy's tiny clothes were strewn down the steps.

Huh?

Becky had followed me out, with Lily on her hip. "Find her?"

"No, but I found her clothes." I pointed at the small pile.

"Huh," Becky said.

"REMY!" I raised my voice and shouted into the cool Montana night. The moon was full, so I could at least see a little as I scanned the nearby landscape.

"She took off her clothes to be like a wolf," Lily said.

"Ohhh." Becky seemed to understand her daughter better than I did. "Did she want to find her daddy?"

Lily nodded her blonde head. "Yeah. She ran up the mountain."

Oh, shit.

"What?" I tried to keep my voice calm to not scare Lily, but now I was genuinely worried. "Up the mountain?"

Remy ran naked up the mountain? Crap!

Becky's voice matched my tension. "Okay, she couldn't have gotten far. Let me get the others, and we'll split up and find her."

"Right." I dashed in to grab my phone to use the flashlight, and the other women came in from the back lawn.

"I should call Wes," I said, dialing his number.

"I, uh, don't think they have reception where they are," Audrey said. "We might be on our own with this for a little while, but we'll find her. She can't have gotten far."

"Right. Lily only came out a minute ago," Becky agreed, pasting on a nervous smile. "Probably right after Remy left."

"No, I watched the movie for a while," Lily said. "She left before the mice started dancing."

I fought panic, running outside. "REMY!"

"Which way did she go, Lils?" Becky asked her daughter, staying right beside me.

I waited for the child to point, and then we both headed off in that direction.

"Marina and I will go this way," Audrey said, pointing off to the right. "Riley, you and Emma go that way." She pointed to the left of the direction Becky and I were headed.

"I'll get on a horse," Charlie offered. "I can ride out to try to find the guys to get them on the hunt, too."

"I'll come with you," Natalie said.

Remy was fine. Remy was fine, I told myself.

Just like she'd been perfectly safe, eating a popsicle on my porch when Wes couldn't find her on moving day. Right now, she was probably perfectly safe.

Then again, she was naked on a mountain at night. The weather was good, no chance of storms like the past few nights, and it was warm. But the odds of her getting lost or bitten by a rattlesnake or...

No, I had to stop.

I couldn't think that way. We'd find her.

My chest constricted with love for the girl. The memory of her falling asleep against me, her happy chatter with my mom last night, and the giant hugs she gave me every time she saw me made my eyes mist up.

But there was no reason to cry. She was fine! Fine! We'd find her.

"Remy!" I called out.

I heard Audrey and Marina calling to the right, and Emma and Riley calling out to our left. The sound of hoof-beats rushed past us, as Natalie and Charlie took the trail up the side of the mountain.

"Remy?" My heart was in my throat, my stomach a tight

ball. It was getting hard to breathe. The more minutes passed without us finding her, the more freaked out I got.

"One of us should have stayed back," I realized, stopping for a moment. "You go back," I told Becky because carrying a two-year-old on a nighttime hike was probably more difficult than she made it look. "In case she's actually still at the house or returns there."

"Good thinking," Becky said, nodding. "Give me your number, and I'll call if I see anything or she's really hiding or something."

"Oh God, I don't have everyone's numbers!" My fingers shook as I opened my phone screen to enter her number in my phone.

"I'll send a group text, so you get everyone's," Becky reassured me. "I have it up already. Just tell me your number."

I gave her the digits followed by a quick tense hug before we parted ways. Once alone, it was even harder to stay positive.

Remy could be hurt. Lost.

What if we didn't find her before something terrible happened?

What if...oh God! What if her mom had come out to the ranch and kidnapped her?

No, that wouldn't be it. Lily had said she wanted to run with the wolves. She would've mentioned if she'd left with someone.

I kept hiking and calling Remy's name until I was hoarse.

In the distance, I heard the howl of a wolf.

Hairs rose on my arms. When a chorus of other wolves

answered the howl, I got downright scared. What if that was a victory cry from a hunt?

What if the hunt had netted them a four-year-old girl?

My knees buckled in fear. "Remy?" I screamed. "REMY! Where are you?"

22

WES

ROB'S DISTINCT howl was a summons, and we all stopped and made our way to him. The moment I caught the scent of horses, I knew something was wrong. The women must've ridden up here because something happened. There was no other reason for them to do so. They knew it was a distraction, and it also made the horses skittish.

I raced to the crest where Rob stood, in human form, with Charlie and Natalie.

"Remy's out on the mountain," he said tersely, not waiting for me to shift. "She said she wanted to run with the wolves. The women are trying to find her. You go now, I'll send the rest after you."

I wheeled around and raced down the mountain, my paws scrabbling on the rocks with my speed. I stopped when I heard the call of voices. It was the women, calling

Remy's name. I pricked my ears, listening for my daughter's answer.

There.

I wasn't sure whether I heard her voice out loud, or if it was just wolf instinct guiding me, but I was certain which direction to go.

I turned and galloped down the mountain. The frantic sound of Joy's voice calling Remy's name grew louder. My mate was on the right trail, too.

Of course, she was. Because she was my mate. Human or not, she had instincts for her pup. And, yes, I now believed Remy was Joy's pup, even after less than a week of knowing her. She had more love for my daughter and took more responsibility for her care than Soraya ever showed.

But I couldn't think about Remy's biological mom right now.

That was a separate cluster fuck.

Right now I had to find Remy.

"Joy!"

There.

I heard it–my daughter's voice. The sound was weak and thin, but I was sure it was her. I stopped only long enough to howl and let the pack know I was on her trail, then charged in the direction of her voice.

"Remy?" Joy had heard her, too. "Where are you, baby? I'm coming!"

I skidded to the edge of a crevice and peered over the ledge. My little girl was down at the bottom. Naked, except for her little sandals.

Fate had to help me.

I lifted my snout to the moon and howled, letting the pack know I'd found her.

"Daddy!" Remy shouted, recognizing my wolf. She waved her little arms. "I'm down here!"

"I see you, Remy!" Joy was already skidding and sliding down the opposite edge of the drop-off. Shit, she could get hurt!

I leaped down to the ledge below me, then another, taking the sheer cliff face in small bites until I was down.

I raced to Remy, and she threw her arms around my neck and started crying.

"Remy–don't move!" For a brief moment, I couldn't understand the tension and fear in Joy's voice.

Then I realized. She was afraid of *me*.

Her own mate.

She hadn't seen me in wolf form. Still didn't know what I was.

The yips of my packmates arriving and gathering on the ridge above only added to Joy's fear. She shot a quick glance at them as she stooped to pick up a large rock, advancing slowly toward us with stealth. She gripped the rock out in front of her body, as if ready to use it.

"Slowly move away from the wolf, Remy," Joy warned her. Her voice was calm and steady, but I heard the thread of fear. Sweat dotted her face, and her eyes were wild. She weighed the rock in her hand like a softball.

"I don't want to," Remy whined, not understanding why she should leave her father.

"It's okay. Come toward me," Joy beckoned with her free hand, still creeping toward us.

Then she wound up, just like a softball pitcher, and

hurled the rock at me. I had to dodge to the side to avoid getting hit in the head. If it were anyone else, I'd be pissed. But I was proud of my fierce mate. She had hidden talents!

Remy screamed. "Stop it!" She threw her arms around my neck. "Don't hurt my daddy."

"Remy!" Joy cried out in alarm.

Fuck it. I didn't care if Rob and the entire pack were watching me break pack rules. Joy was my mate. I wasn't going to let her go. But I had no idea what she'd do to protect Remy from a supposed threat. I already had a rock come at me. I could survive it, but if she got more desperate, she might do something rash and get hurt. And hurt Remy with her.

I was all in with her, and we were going to figure out how to be together as a shifter, a shifter pup, and a human, or I'd die trying.

That meant she needed to know what I was.

I shifted and stood beside Remy.

Joy screamed and stumbled backward, landing on her ass.

"It's okay. It's me." I lunged forward and lifted her to stand, pulling her roughly against my body. She was shaking and sweaty and breathing hard.

In my periphery, I saw my pack wolves slinking away to give us privacy. "I won't hurt you."

Joy gaped up at me and then, like the time she had giggled in the middle of her tears, she laughed. "Wes?" Her smile was broad, like this was some funny coincidence meeting out here on the mountain with me buck naked, having just changed forms.

"You're... you're not scared?"

"Of *you*?" She laughed some more, throwing her arms around me. "Why would I be scared of you?"

Remy wrapped her little arms around Joy's waist from the back.

"Um, you know. Because of the wolf thing?" I ruffled Remy's hair, then stepped back to hoist her into my arms, so I knew she was safe.

Joy included her in our little circle and started laughing for real. "You're a wolf."

Laughter seemed to be her default when she needed to get emotions out of her body. Laughter or sex. She definitely didn't prefer crying, but I'd help her with that. I wanted her to feel safe expressing all her emotions, even the sadder ones.

She'd have excess adrenaline in her body later, and I could definitely fuck it out of her again. For now, though, I'd hold her. Hold *both* my girls.

"Daddy's a wolf!" Remy cried proudly. Then she turned to me, clapped her little hands against my cheeks. "I wanted to run with you tonight, Daddy."

"Yeah, baby, that was a problem." Shifters were used to seeing each other naked, so Remy didn't notice the state of my undress. "You can't shift yet. Not until you hit puberty when you're bigger. A lot bigger. Until then, you have to stay back with the humans on the full moon runs. You know this."

She sighed. "But I wanted to *see* the wolves."

I glanced up at Joy. I had so much to explain to her. "Well, we didn't show you tonight because Joy didn't know we were wolves. Remember how we've talked about it being a secret?"

"But Joy's one of us," Remy insisted, nodding her head. Her hair was snarled, and her face had dirt smudges on it.

For some reason, that made my eyes smart. I looked at my beautiful mate, wrapping my arm tighter about her waist. "She is. At least I hope she will be."

Joy had tears in her eyes, too. "I don't know what that means." She was laughing again. "Are you asking if you can turn me into a wolf or something?"

It was my turn to laugh—a foreign sound that rocketed from my throat and surprised me.

That made Joy giggle more. And Remy.

I shook my head. "No, honey. I just want you to be my mate. Keep our pack secret. Carry my scent."

"Um...okay." There was still laughter in Joy's voice.

I wasn't sure she was taking this seriously or understood what she was getting herself into, but I'd explain it all when we were back home. Right now I needed to get my two females out of this gully and off the mountain.

As if to punctuate that thought, Remy whined, "I wanna go home."

"Climb on my back, baby, and I'll take my girls home." I said before I dropped to all fours and shifted into wolf form. Remy was on my back and Joy followed along beside me as I took the direct way back to the ranch house. And then we'd go home.

23

JOY

WES WAS A WOLF. A *giant* black wolf.

A WOLF.

A wolf with green eyes that glinted in the moonlight. I'd seen those green wolf eyes showing through before but never, ever imagined the secret he carried.

I was still trying to digest it all. The fact that my new neighbor–my new boyfriend–was actually a *wolf*. It didn't make sense, but I'd seen it with my own eyes.

It was real.

Remy'd had her arms around the wolf one second–which was crazy enough in itself–and then he was suddenly Wes. Poof! Or pop! Or... groan? Remy wasn't surprised at all by her father being a wolf, turning back to... human. She was calm because she knew. Four-year-olds were fine with crazy things if it was normal. They didn't know it *wasn't* normal.

Other clues I'd missed came rushing in. She'd said she wanted to go run with the wolves. That made much more sense when I understood her *dad* was one of the wolves. She'd also called her mom a wolf. What had she said when Soraya had come to the house? *I don't like her, even if she is a wolf.*

I wondered how she'd known. She sure didn't look like anything more than a bitch to me. Was there something in a... a shifter's appearance I should look for? Like the way I'd seen Wes' eyes glint green? I'd thought it had been a trick of the light.

There had to be more than an eye thing. Right?

As we headed back to Rob and Willow's ranch house, I walked beside Wes, admiring what a beautiful animal he was–the thick, glossy black coat, the broad, muscled shoulders moving gracefully as he traveled on powerful legs. Damn, his wolf was actually big enough for a child to ride on his back like a horse!

My mind shifted to the ring of wolves standing along the edge of the gully. They'd showed up right after Wes.

God, were the guys on the ranch wolves, too? They had to be. Were they all out... running together?

And why?

The women had, well, lied and said the men were moving cattle. Cattle, my ass. That meant they knew. Of course, they did. They were either dating or married.

I'd lived in Cooper Valley my whole life, and I'd never realized Wolf Ranch was a *literal* ranch of wolves! They'd done a really good job keeping it a secret.

Everyone was out on the front porch waiting for us, going right to Remy and giving her hugs and lots of tons of attention as a no-longer-a-wolf-but-naked Wes disappeared to pull on his clothes, wherever he'd left them.

"I'll bet you have questions," Marina said to me, pulling me aside. "I'm sorry we lied, but it's not a little secret."

"The secret is out, and I'm gonna answer anything Joy can think of," Wes growled, coming up behind us. He wrapped a strong arm around my waist and kissed my temple. "Are you okay?" he murmured. He was sweaty and streaked with dirt. There was even a twig in his hair. "Freaking out?"

"I'm...no, I'm okay." I bobbed my head. I wasn't freaking out. I was more fascinated. Curious. Dying to know more.

"Well, if you need to talk about it tomorrow, call me," Marina offered. "It was a secret for me, too. I know what it's like to find out your boyfriend is another species who wants to mark you as his forever mate."

I blinked. "He what now?"

"You're not helping," Wes growled at Marina. His brows were down low, in his typical grouchy face, but I sensed it was because he was worried about how I was taking it. He kept shooting me searching looks.

"If it's okay, I'm gonna give Remy a quick rinse since she's filthy, and she'll no doubt fall asleep on the way home," Wes said.

"Of course," Marina replied. "I'll grab one of my shirts for her to wear like a nightgown."

We didn't talk as I helped Wes get a tired and now cranky Remy into the tub for the world's fastest bath, and we put her in Marina's shirt and climbed in the truck. As expected, she fell asleep even before Wes pulled onto the dirt road.

"Tell me." I took his hand that rested on his thigh and moved our joined fingers to mine.

He sent me another one of those searching looks as he drove. "Well, you now know I'm a shifter."

"So is everyone at Wolf Ranch?"

"Most everyone." He squeezed my fingers. "Tonight was a full moon, and we have the need to run beneath it. It's a pack tradition to get together every month for it. Everyone who stayed behind is human."

I named everyone just to make sure. "Marina, Charlie, Natalie, Emma, Riley, and Audrey. Oh... and Becky."

"That's right. They're all mated to shifters."

"Mated. Like... married?"

"Like fate put them together. The guys knew their mate by scent."

I gasped, having one more thing make sense. "That's why Soraya sniffed me!"

Wes' lips turned up for a second. "Yes. She was seeing if you were a wolf."

"She's a wolf–Remy had said that after Soraya came by that night, but I didn't understand what she meant."

He nodded. "Yes."

"So that means Remy's a wolf."

"Yes. But she won't shift until puberty."

I shook my head in disbelief. "Amazing."

I didn't know why Wes had thought I'd freak out. I couldn't be more thrilled. It was like finding out magic was real.

Wes glanced over at me. "You think it's amazing?"

"I think it's incredible." I remembered how he looked as a giant black wolf. "You're incredible."

"You're not over there losing your shit while faking being okay?"

I laughed. He had me all figured out. "No, not faking. Should I be losing my shit?"

"No, honey. Well, there are a couple of things I haven't explained yet."

"Only a couple?"

It was his turn to laugh, which was a rich, deep sound I loved. "Fine. A lot more than–"

I gasped as I had a lightbulb moment. "You heal quickly, don't you?"

He flicked his gaze to mine then back on the road. "Yes. That was why I panicked with you up on your roof. If I fell off, it'd hurt like a bitch, but I'd be fine in a matter of minutes. If something happened to you–fuck. I'd never forgive myself."

"That's why Remy's little cut healed up!"

He turned to look at me, confused.

"That night I watched Remy, she was doing clay, and she poked herself with one of my tools. There was a little blood, but it healed before I could even find BandAids in your bathroom."

"I don't have any."

Huh. That must be nice.

We pulled into his driveway and parked. The silence of the night settled over us.

I looked to Wes. He looked to me.

There was something different in the air now. Not a scent or anything but a feeling. Knowing his huge secret, I felt like we were closer. Like there were less barriers between understanding each other. Between knowing who we really were.

"What are the things you haven't explained yet?" I asked. I wanted to know everything.

Things with Wes were new, but I was already committed. Everything about him felt right, including his adorable daughter and that wonderful group of people I'd spent the evening with.

"What Marina mentioned–about marking you as my forever mate?" His voice was tentative, as if broaching a tricky subject.

"Yeah, what does that mean?"

"Wolf shifters can have what you would call normal relationships. They can date. Some follow human traditions and legally marry. They have families–all that. But there's also the potential for finding their fated mate–what you might call 'the one.'"

I tried and failed to swallow. For some inexplicable reason, my heart started to beat hard against my ribs.

What was he saying?

"The story goes that a wolf will recognize his fated mate by her scent. You don't know what that means until you experience it. At least I didn't." His eyes glowed green in the darkness.

I was seeing his wolf eyes. Was he saying–

"Am I... am I your mate?" I whispered.

He brought our still-joined hands to his mouth and kissed my knuckles once more. "Yes. I should have known the second I caught your scent, but I was all riled up about Remy being missing. Your scent sent me into, well, a ravenous fit of lust, but at the time, I didn't know it was because you're my mate."

I laughed again. "Ravenous fit of lust?"

His eyes narrowed, and his voice went deeper. "What would you call it then? How we came together. I remember you on your knees for me."

I swallowed hard. It was a night I'd never forget.

"Fit of lust works," I squeaked, squirming in my seat.

My panties were wet for another round of him being ravenous.

"Now, honey, I want you to be mine. I want you to be my mate."

The idea of it thrilled me, but I still didn't understand completely. "What does that mean exactly?"

"Male wolves mark their fated mates with a mating bite. It permanently embeds their scent into the female, so all other wolves know she's been claimed."

"Claimed? Sounds a little sexist," I teased, while recognizing I was getting wetter and wetter the longer this conversation continued.

Wes' lips twitched. I loved seeing even the start of a smile on his handsome face. "Male wolves are very territorial. If you're at least marked, it allows my wolf to calm some of his aggression trying to keep other males away from you. The other day when I asked Colton and Johnny to help with your roof, I wanted to kill them both for being near you."

I laughed. "You did?"

The two men were attractive, but they had nothing on Wes.

"Honey, when a wolf has a mate, he'll do anything in

the world to protect her, provide for her, and keep the other males away from her."

I smiled. I kind of loved knowing he felt territorial over me. It gave me a sense of feminine power to know he thought I was worth defending.

I held up my free hand. "Um, also, did you say *bite*?"

Wes flashed a grin–a real one. A ravenous one. His eyes glowed bright green. "That's right, honey." His voice had a deep, throaty rumble, like he was turned on. Like biting me would be the sexiest thing we'd done yet. Well, it would.

My pulse raced. A thrum built between my legs.

"Show me?" I breathed.

He nodded, and we slipped from the truck. Wes lifted Remy from her car seat and carried her to bed. Then he led me to the shower.

24

WES

REMY MIGHT HAVE BEEN clean from her quick bath, but Joy and I were both filthy. Dirt and little bits of leaves were stuck in Joy's clothes. Since I ran naked, my body looked like I rolled around in a mud puddle. Then, got sweaty.

Yet twigs and all, she was the most beautiful thing I'd ever seen. So I told her that. "Honey, you're fucking gorgeous."

I grabbed the hem of her dirty t-shift and lifted.

She blushed furiously, but I could see from her eyes that she liked the praise. Her mother was a kind woman, but needy. I had to wonder if she gave her daughter encouragement and reminded her of her worth often enough.

I would. Every day of her life.

"Do shifters have problems with their eyesight?" she asked, her lips quirking, obviously not thinking to herself that she was pretty.

Reaching up, I pulled a blade of grass from her hair. "You went after Remy, not thinking of yourself or the danger you could be in."

To prove it, I ran a finger along a scratch on her forearm. An angry raised red line. I hated to see one bit of damage to her beautiful body. "Does this hurt?"

She shook her head.

"Hurt anywhere else?"

"No, but I'll probably feel it tomorrow."

She stood before me in her bra and shorts. Shoes and socks.

"I'm gonna get you bare and check over every inch of you." *Then fuck you until you forget your name and scream mine.*

She swallowed, and I couldn't miss the thrum of her pulse at her neck. The spot I wanted to bite but knew I might mark her a few inches lower.

"Okay."

Reaching into the shower, I turned on the spray to let it warm up.

Then I focused on my mate. I dropped to my knees before her, undid her shorts, and pushed them down. When I untangled them from her feet, I took her shoes and socks off with them.

"Fuck, you're mine. I can't believe how perfect you are." I kissed her belly. Tasted her salty sweat. Breathed in her tangy scent from her exertion, plus the sweet musk of her arousal.

"Wes." She tangled her fingers in my hair. She paused and pulled something from it. A twig.

She smiled.

I couldn't help but smile back. My pup was safe and asleep in her bed. My mate was almost bare to me. With a flick of my wrist, the back clasp of her bra opened then the simple but still sexy garment slid down her arms.

My control was slowly slipping away, but this time I had to take it slow. I wanted to savor every inch of her.

With fingers hooked into the elastic and a quick tug, her panties were around her ankles.

With gentle fingers, I skimmed my hands over her. Even spinning her around, so I could take in her back.

From my position on my knees, I kissed her full butt cheek.

She stiffened with a little gasp.

"I'm not biting you here," I murmured, gripping her hips and spinning her around once again. "Mmm, here would be nice." My mouth was just above her trimmed pussy hair.

"Wes," she breathed.

The bathroom filled with steam. It was time to get my girl all clean, so I could get filthy with her. And make her mine.

JOY

I THOUGHT he was going to fuck me in the shower. It was definitely on my to-do list for places to have sex with Wes. Instead, he'd washed me, head to toe. Shampooed and conditioned my hair. Kissed and let his fingers run all over as he circled me to make sure I didn't have any other scratches besides the one on my arm.

Then he quickly soaped up and rinsed off and helped me out.

Who knew sexy shower time was the best foreplay?

Wes licked and kissed his way down my body some more as he toweled me dry, leaving me trembling under his touch—every nerve activated and sensitized to his touch, his breath, his growls of approval.

I was in a delicious haze of not only lust, but something even more intoxicating—the idea of getting serious with Wes.

Being claimed by this burly, grumpy cinnamon roll dad. A man who wanted to bite me and mark me as his. God, it felt beyond romantic. It felt natural and right.

Maybe I had abandonment issues from my dad moving out. Maybe it was from the fear of losing my mom every time she struggled.

Or maybe it was simply that I felt what Wes did–that he was "the one." Fate had interceded when it chose Wes to move next door.

As an artist, I'd trusted in fate. When I first started throwing pots and wanted to make a living out of it, I put it out to the Universe. I figured if it was meant to be, they'd sell. If I earned enough from the pottery to quit my job slinging beer at Cody's, that would be a sign I was on the right path. Over time, I'd been able to quit my job.

I wasn't making six figures or anything, but I made enough for a down payment on my house. I made enough to make it a full-time gig.

Therefore, I believed now that fate had brought me the one man made for me. The one who I "fit" with. Who got me. Who I felt at home with from the first moment I saw him, even when he was being a grouchy ass.

Was it fast? Yes. Ridiculously so. If a friend of mine said she met a guy the other day, they were in love, and wanted to get his name tattooed permanently on her body, I'd tell her to pump those brakes.

Except, I just... knew, and I didn't have an inner wolf or a super scenter.

I just wanted Wes. And Remy.

Wes dropped the towel to the floor and scooped me up into his arms.

"Mine," he growled as he carried me to his bedroom.

My pussy clenched. I absolutely *loved* that assertion.

I loved the idea of being his. I wanted him to be mine in return.

I tried on the idea of moving in here with him permanently. Of co-parenting Remy. Of giving her siblings.

It all felt perfect.

I could turn my house into an entire art studio. Maybe I could even use the living area as a "showroom" and sell directly from my house.

I was getting ahead of myself.

Maybe I should pump those brakes in my mind.

Wes laid me on my back and studied my face. "Now you're freaking out."

"Not freaking out," I admitted as I shook my head. "Just wondered if it's going too fast."

He traced his fingertip around my nipple. "You don't have to be afraid of anything. Not with me. If you want me to wait to mark you, I will. I'll spend every day for the rest of my life proving to you that I'm worthy of being your mate, if that's what it takes. I just want you near me. Part of our lives."

My eyes misted up, and I reached for his face, pulling him down for a kiss. "It's not that, I just..."

He straddled my waist, gently manacling my wrists and pinning them beside my head. I loved feeling trapped by him. Trapped meant safe. "Tell me."

I arched my tits up, wanting more of his touch because the position he had me in turned me on.

"Tell me everything you're afraid of. Let's get it all out on the table, so we know what we're dealing with."

I hesitated. I wasn't sure if my fears had names or were even rational.

"I'll go first," he said. "I'm scared the wolf thing will freak you out. That you'll decide it's not for you. I'm scared you'll find it too much with me being a package deal with Remy." He glanced away for a second then back. "And... I'm scared Remy will get hurt. That she'll get attached to you, and then if things don't work out, it will break her heart even more than having a mom who broke her heart."

My eyes teared up for him. For Remy. For the moment of vulnerability. He was so incredible and brave to share with me. His fears were reasonable and made sense.

He seemed to realize it was not the moment for bondage because he released my wrists and let me wrap my arms around his neck to hold him.

It was easier to talk with my lips against his neck, my face hidden. "I'm afraid...I don't know–that I'm being impulsive or irrational. That if things don't work out, people will judge me for rushing in. I know that's stupid to worry about what other people think, but–"

His thumb stroked my cheek. "It's not stupid. I get it. What else? I want to hear every last reservation."

"Okay..." This suddenly became a game we were in together instead of a crisis of big decisions.

Wes settled us on our sides, facing each other, then ensured the blanket was pulled up over our bare skin.

"What if you're catfishing me?" I giggled at the absurdity of the idea. I'd known Rob and Boyd Wolf and most of the guys on the ranch forever. Wes was one of their friends. He wasn't some rando guy making a play for me with an ulterior motive. But just saying it out loud cleared any shadow of worry I had.

Wes chuckled, too. "I'm *definitely* catfishing you. I want access to all your gorgeous pottery and keep it for myself."

I couldn't help but giggle again.

"What if you're a narcissist who lures me in with hot sex and handyman favors until I'm locked in and then starts controlling and gaslighting?" As I said those words, I knew they were impossible. I'd seen him with his daughter. He wasn't a narcissist. He was the opposite.

He didn't seem offended. "What else do you have?"

I let my mind go to the very worst fear. Maybe the one every woman on the planet had to be cautious about. "What if you turn into an abuser, and then I'm locked in a wolf cult that won't let me out?"

Wes went very still, eyes wide. "Fuck, Joy. That's some seriously scary shit." He didn't speak or move quickly to reassure me. He just let that fear shimmer between us before it drifted away, out the window.

Then he said carefully, "Abuse can happen in wolf communities, same as human ones. But I've never heard of it in a fated match. My body is literally wired to please yours. Your pleasure is mine. Your survival is mine. Your tears will instantly lower my aggression if I caused them or raise it if someone else has. I was born to love you. I won't ever let anyone hurt you. I would die to protect you. I will live to satisfy you–sexually, emotionally, and physically. And if some day, satisfying you meant letting you go–if you ever wanted your freedom–honey, I would give it to you. Even if it killed me to do so."

The intensity of the moment felt like it would crack

open my chest. I neither wanted to cry, nor giggle, even more to let it out. I just held the sensation in my heart. In my chest. It was the feeling of being vulnerable with a man. Of learning to trust another person to take care of my needs when people had failed in the past.

Was that what I was truly afraid of? Being hurt by the one who I now trusted the most?

And then, because we were being real, I decided to share those thoughts out loud. "I think what I'm really scared of is the same thing you're afraid of for Remy." Tears swam in my eyes. "My parents' marriage didn't work out, and it was painful for all three of us. I guess I'm scared that I'll learn to trust and then get hurt. I know what it's like for the child, and I wouldn't want that for Remy either."

Wes leaned his forehead against mine. "I guess there are no guarantees, right? I feel that way about Remy every day. Like–I love this kid so much and if anything ever happened–if I ever lost her for some reason–I don't know if I could go on." Wes blinked hard, like his eyes were smarting. I wondered if he was thinking about how she'd run off earlier.

A tear leaked from my eye, but I didn't care. I didn't need to avoid the tears or the pain. We were facing our deepest darkness together.

Together.

"I want this," I said with total clarity.

There were no guarantees. Even if we lived our lives out together in a perfect "happily ever after," one of us would die first. Someone would have a broken heart. It was the inevitability of living. We all had hearts that broke, and we all were going to die. Nothing could protect us from either of those things, and the more we tried to stop them, the less we lived. The less we loved. The less we enjoyed this life we were given.

"I want you," Wes said. His dick hardened against my belly, and his eyes glowed green, but he waited. I could see the hunger in them, but he didn't pounce.

"Can we go back to that part where you pin me down and have your ravenous way with me?" I asked.

Wes' smile was brilliant.

The most blinding thing I'd ever seen.

It registered as pure pleasure in me because I'd caused it. I was the source of his joy.

In a breathtaking swoop, he flipped me on my back and manacled my wrists above my head once again. "Now you're in trouble, little human," he growled.

I squirmed beneath him, thrills of heat pulsing through me.

"Show me," I dared him.

26

WES

I COULDN'T WAIT A SECOND LONGER to make her mine. I lowered my head and sucked on one of Joy's nipples as I rolled the other between my thumb and forefinger. My wolf was already ravenous for her. My teeth had sharpened. My dick throbbed.

The scent of her swirled around us. The feel of her beneath me was soft, warm, and plush. She was safe. Protected. Cared for. I'd said the words, now it was time to prove it to her with action.

Yet I was going to take my time doing so. This was about giving, not taking. I was going to teach Joy what she could expect from me. My full attention to her pleasure. My time and focus. My love.

Fate, we hadn't even said we loved each other. That was probably more important to her, as a human, than hearing I wanted to mark her.

So I started where I was. Words weren't my thing, but Joy needed to hear mine. I had to give her all of me, even the hard parts. I'd start with something easy. "I love this nipple," I said, then switched to suck the other one. "And I love this one." I gave it the same treatment then dragged my open mouth down her belly, nipping at her side and making her giggle.

I traced her navel. "I love this belly button."

I kissed down to the apex of her slit, where I nudged my tongue in. "I love your little clit." I flicked the tip of my tongue over that swollen little pearl, then rolled it around. I traced down her inner lips. "I love this delicious pussy."

I penetrated her with my tongue. "I love the honey you make for me."

Joy's ass clenched, and her inner thighs clamped around my ears. She gushed fresh arousal down my chin.

"You're fucking gorgeous." I lifted my head to watch her face as I penetrated her with two fingers, my thumb rubbing over her clit.

She shook beneath me, releasing in a mini-climax.

"I love your orgasms." I found her G-spot and circled it deep inside her.

She whimpered at the sensation. "Yes," she moaned. "Please."

"Tell me what you need, Joy."

Her skin was hot, her breath ragged, her body pliant. "I need...your cock."

"You want this cock?" I slid my fingers out and licked her juices from them, then rose up on my knees. Her taste on my tongue was heaven.

"Yes!" She reached with her legs, and her feet hooked behind my back to tug my hips down to hers.

I renewed my hold on her manacled wrists with one hand and with the other, gripped my cock to rub the head over her soft folds.

"Give me that big wolf cock."

Oh damn. Joy could dirty-talk as well as I could. It made me spurt pre-cum.

"I want you inside me."

My canines dropped, wolf roaring. I nearly came right then, before I even got inside her tight tunnel.

"Fuck me, Wes."

Fate help me–I was going to *devour* her. Hunger to claim her ripped through me.

I speared her with my erection in one long instroke. She gasped as I slammed into the hilt.

I forced myself to hold still in case it had been too much or she needed time to adjust. "Like that, honey?"

She rocked her hips to move me inside her. She was dripping wet, which eased my way. "Yes. Fuck me now. Claim me."

A growl shot out of my throat, and I started fucking her in earnest, plowing in and out, giving it to her fast and hard. The bed slammed against the wall.

"Yes," she moaned, rolling her hips up to meet mine. "Please, Wes."

Fuck.

I was a goner.

She was killing me. I held her by the nape to keep from driving her head into the headboard as I drilled into her.

"Yes...yes!" she screamed.

I couldn't wait any longer. My wolf was beyond ready. I had to have her. Had to claim her as mine. Forever.

"Come for me, honey," I growled.

"Yes! Okay!" she cried.

I plunged deep and came, spilling hot ribbons of cum into her.

She obeyed my command, her muscles clenching around my dick, spasming in her glorious release. Each squeeze milked my dick for more cum. Each tremor pumped more up from my balls.

The instinct to sink my teeth deep into her flesh blinded me, but I held back. She was human–she would certainly scar from this and possibly be seriously injured if I wasn't careful.

As both of us neared the end of the orgasm, I rocked slowly in and out to wring more pleasure from her. "Where do you want it?"

She looked confused at first, still dazed from the orgasm.

"May I bite you?"

She held my gaze and nodded, mouth open like she was turned on. She pointed at her breast.

I cupped it. "Here?"

"Yes."

My cock lengthened inside her. I had to twist to get my head to her breast, but I did it.

Careful–careful! I warned my wolf.

Just a little nip. My four canines framed the top outer edge of her breast and sank in, piercing the flesh. I came again, shuddering with the intense pleasure of marking my mate.

Joy had cried out, and I stopped myself before I went too deep, very gently easing my teeth from her flesh to keep from tearing her delicate tissues.

I pulled out, suddenly horrified at the thought of her pain. I licked the wounds because my saliva would promote her healing. I looked up her body and met her gaze. "Are you okay? Fuck. I'm so sorry, how bad does it hurt?"

Joy's face was flushed, her eyes glassy. She reached a hand between her legs and rubbed her clit.

I watched, entranced by my beautiful mate bringing herself to a third orgasm. Even though blood trickled from the puncture wounds in her breast, she didn't appear to be in agony.

She was experiencing pleasure–same as I had.

As she rubbed between her legs and then gasped, hips lifting from the bed, I watched and took a mental picture, wanting to save this incredible moment in my memory banks forever.

When I was sure I had it, I pushed her fingers away and lowered my head. If my mate wanted more pleasure, I was sure as hell going to deliver it.

All night long.

27

JOY

Because of the crazy night, Remy slept late. So did we. In fact, we didn't stir until she came in and climbed into bed with us. She didn't comment that I'd slept in her father's bed again or that we were naked. No, she commented on Marina's t-shirt she was wearing and how she loved it and wanted to wear it all day. The mind of a four-year-old was so sweet and simple.

Thirty minutes later, Remy and I were outside on the back deck eating bowls of yogurt with granola and fruit. I'd put on my old jean cutoffs and tank top against the heat and because I was going to work in my studio for most of the day. Remy was still in the t-shirt. Her "fancy dress."

Wes was inside starting a new pot of coffee.

The back door was open. The sun was shining. Birds were chirping. I felt like my life was like a Disney movie. Maybe I was the princess that Remy spoke of.

I got my prince. I set my hand over the spot on my breast where Wes bit me. God, it sounded like we were into kinky shit. Maybe, being all hot for a guy who turned into a wolf was the ultimate kink. No, it was letting him bite me. Mark me–because when I'd put my bra on earlier, I saw the red marks of the puncture wound. It didn't hurt although when I pressed on the spot it *was* a little bruised.

So was my pussy from being railed into the headboard.

Both made me smile.

"I like this crunchy stuff in my gurt." Remy said, waving her spoon around and pulling me from my thoughts.

"Granola," I said. She repeated the word, but it came out as "grola."

Whatever.

A cell phone chimed from inside. It wasn't mine, and Remy was four, so it had to be Wes'.

"Yeah?" The sound of that one word was rough and unpleasant. Like he knew who the caller was and spared no good attitude on them.

"What? Why?"

I stared at Remy who was busy spooning up more of her breakfast, who didn't even notice her father was now cranky.

I booped her on the nose as I stood, and she giggled.

In the kitchen, Wes was leaning against the counter in jeans and a snap shirt. I went to him, and he tucked his arm around me.

"I've talked to my region's Shifter Council member. He agrees Remy is mine, so I'm coming to get her tomorrow morning."

Oh God. *Remy was hers?* Was this Soraya?

"You're not getting my daughter, Soraya" he snarled, confirming my suspicions.

His hold loosened, and he stepped away, pacing the room.

I glanced out the back door and saw Remy happily talking to herself. She was on her knees at the table, not ten feet away. She was safe.

"*Our* daughter," I heard through the phone.

"Why are you doing this?" he demanded. "Why the *fuck* are you doing this now?"

She gave a humorless laugh. "Because you're with a human."

I sucked in a breath and met Wes' green gaze.

Me. Soraya wanted her daughter because she wanted the child away from me.

Me. This was happening because of me. Tears smarted my eyes.

Soraya showed up *after* the storm. After I moved into Wes' house. Wolves were possessive about their mates and pups–so even if she didn't want Wes, it probably pissed her off to have me around. It was my fault. If I'd stayed at my place, she would never have known Wes and I were dating.

"What the fuck does that have to do with anything?"

Wes didn't swear in front of Remy. I hadn't really heard him swear that much at all. This definitely was a bad word moment, though. I wanted to grab the phone from his hands and give her a few choice words. But I'd lose. Because she had the edge here. I *was* human.

"I won't have my *shifter* daughter *tainted* by a *human*. What is she going to teach her? How is she going to help her grow into a strong and powerful shifter female?"

His gaze flicked to mine then out the door to Remy.

I did the same, staring between the two.

"How have *you* been teaching her anything these past four years?" he countered.

"I'm starting now."

"You're *not* taking her."

"You're shacking up with a *human*. I *am* taking her. I already have the council behind me. I'm the mother, and it's agreed Remington isn't in an environment where she can thrive."

Wes' eyes widened, and he tugged at his hair. He spun in a circle and stopped right in front of the back door, so he could stare at his child.

This was heartbreaking to watch. To hear someone ready to rip Wes' daughter from him. God, he'd told me last night that losing Remy was his biggest fear.

I couldn't let that happen.

"I'll be there tomorrow morning at ten. Someone from the council will be with me to ensure you comply."

With that, the call ended.

Wes threw his phone onto the granite counter, and it skidded across the surface with a clatter.

Soraya was a bitch. I didn't like to use that term too often, but like the swearing, this was the appropriate time. The reason swear-words existed was for the purpose of catharsis. I never expected everyone to be my friend. That was fine. But she hated me. I'd said only a few sentences with her, and with one sniff, she hated my guts.

She was forcing Wes to choose between me and his daughter.

It was horrible.

I was afraid to touch him; he seemed like he was ready to erupt. As if his wolf needed to come out and run or fight or something.

"Can she do this?" I whispered.

He stared at Remy, scrubbing a hand across his red beard. "Yes," he spat. "If she really has the council involved."

"What *is* the council?" I wondered, my shaky fingers going to my lips.

"It's like a governing body. Judges, with members from the biggest packs in the region. They hear intra-pack issues or things that affect our kind as a whole. Their rulings hold. Punishment is dealt with by council enforcers. One of our pack members serves the council as an enforcer–Johnny."

"Johnny?" I asked, stunned. "He's like... twenty-two."

Wes nodded. "It was Clint before him, but he gave up the role after Lily was born."

"So if she's bringing a council person with her, then–"

"Then it won't be Johnny. It will be someone who can speak for the council and whose ruling holds. It means she's taking Remy, and there's nothing I can do to stop it."

"Take her. Run!" I suggested, starting to panic for them. No way was he letting her go with that psycho bitch.

"Rob would have to send Johnny after me. He'd have to" –Wes swallowed hard– "kill me, and he'd be forced to take Remy to Soraya."

"What? All of this because of *me*?"

Wes' face contorted into a dangerous scowl. "Not you. *Her*."

"Then I'll go. We break up. If I'm the problem, we elimi-nate me from the equation. If we're no longer together, then there's no reason for Soraya to give to the council to take Remy away."

Wes spun around to face me. "You're my *mate*," he growled.

I pointed out the back door and let the tears fall. "She's your *daughter*." I swallowed hard and tried to breathe them back, but it wasn't working. "We've known each other less than a week. This–" I waved my hand back and forth between us, "–isn't enough. I won't let Remy suffer between warring parents like I did. And I certainly won't let her be taken from you. I won't be the reason you're ripped apart."

"No." His growl was ferocious. If I didn't already trust him to my bones, I might have been scared.

I shook my head. "No. It's over. You told me last night you'd let me go if I asked. I'm asking you now."

"Joy," he pleaded.

"Just grab the things of mine I have over here and throw them into my yard. That way, when they come, they won't smell me."

"Your house has holes in it!" His hands clenched into fists.

I shrugged. "I'll go to my mom's."

That was the last place I wanted to go, but there was no choice here. This wasn't about me. Remy deserved her dad. Needed him.

I went to him, kissed his cheek, then fled, sobs choking my throat.

I wouldn't risk her for anything. Not even love.

28

WES

Joy left. She ran out the front door. Crying.

My wolf raged. I wanted to beat the walls of my house down. To rampage. To fight for her.

But I had my daughter to think of, too.

Joy or Remy.

Soraya was giving me that choice.

Except Joy had decided for me.

My wolf was freaking the fuck out with her being gone.

Ached. Howled. Prowled.

My vision was shifting between wolf and human, like I was about to spontaneously shift and fight off the threat to my pup and mate.

"Daddy, I got gurt on my shirt!" Remy called, running inside with a dirty spoon and fingers covered in white yogurt.

I sucked in a sharp, harsh breath to regain control. I needed to get my wolf on leash, so I could think.

"Okay, let's get you washed up." My voice sounded hollow to my ears. I got a wet cloth and wiped her down, my moves wooden.

All the light that Joy had brought to my life had drained. Everything was black and white and red. I was... joyless.

Fucking literally.

"Where's Joy?" Remy seemed to read my thoughts.

I cleared my throat, but it didn't remove the sensation of a tight band squeezing the life out of me. "She had to go."

"But she was going to braid my hair," Remy whined.

And she was going to spend her life with me.

Rage built within me again.

How could Soraya do this? Why? Was it really about Joy? I hadn't heard back from Johnny with any updates, but I hadn't cared before. Now? This was a fucking shitshow.

I grabbed my phone that slid behind the toaster.

"Go get your brush and hair ties, and I'll do it after I make a call." I spun her about and gave her a little pat to head toward the bathroom.

Then I dialed my alpha.

"Wolf," Rob said.

"Rob?" My voice was a bark. "I, uh, I need your help." It was hard to get the words out. I was a proud alpha male wolf. I barely communicated with the guys I worked with all day long. Asking for help was out of my wheelhouse, but if ever I needed it, the time was now.

"Name it."

"Remy's mother is coming tomorrow to take Remy. Says

she's bringing a council member to back her up, and they'll uphold it because I'm with a human."

"That's bullshit," Rob growled.

His words gave me a sliver of relief. "Are there laws governing custody?"

"No. If there was an inter-pack dispute, it would be resolved with the council members' decision."

That didn't relieve me at all.

"Soraya had made it sound like the council already made a decision. Without me even presenting my side of the story."

I heard his growl through the phone. Felt it resonate in my chest.

"Maybe she's bringing a council member to make the decision on the spot instead of waiting for their next meeting. It would be unusual, but if time were of the essence, the council might send one member to resolve a dispute like that."

Fuck.

"Did you mark your mate?" he asked.

"Yes." I had to push the image of my beautiful mate's face streaked with tears from my mind because it made me shake with fury at having her taken from me. "Will that play against me?"

"I don't know."

Snakes coiled in my stomach.

"Johnny and I will back you up at the meeting. We don't have a representative on the council, but I'm alpha of a strong pack in the region, and whoever comes should respect my presence. My pack has multiple males mated to humans. If they're going to start to discriminate against us based on that fact, they're going to have problems, and I will make that clear."

"Thank you." I wasn't alone in this. My new pack wouldn't abandon me in my time of need.

"When are they coming?" Rob asked.

"Tomorrow. Ten a.m."

"We'll be there."

"She's gone, Alpha," I added.

"Who?"

The question was valid after Remy ran off the night before. My daughter was a runner, and I had to work on that. Another time.

"Joy. My mate left, so she wouldn't stand between me and my pup."

"Fuck. One thing at a time. We'll take care of Remy, and then you can go after your mate. Come to the ranch now, and Johnny and I will be waiting for you in my office. We'll come up with a plan."

29

JOY

"Hey, Mom." I carried a small suitcase into my mom's house that night.

I'd tried to work in my studio that day–I'd forced myself to because I needed to produce a lot of product to make up for the broken pots–but it was hard to see the clay when the tears kept streaming down my cheeks.

And I wasn't a crier.

I kept telling myself it was foolish to cry over a guy I met a week ago.

Completely absurd.

The fact that he was next door made it even worse. Thankfully the shrubs and some fencing blocked the view as much as my tears.

But my sore breast kept reminding me that it meant so much more than a week of sex. Wes had been serious about me. He believed fate brought us together. That we were meant for each other. That I was "the one."

And damn if he didn't feel like the one for me.

Especially with how much my heart ached at giving him up.

I wasn't going to get in the way of him keeping his daughter, though. I cared way too much about him for that. The thought of Remy going off with that awful woman...

"Joy? What's going on?"

My mom was in the kitchen, which was a good sign. She was in her work clothes, which meant she'd gotten herself out of bed today and gone into the office.

It really had seemed like her visit with Remy had been a reset of sorts for her. It pulled her out of herself. Kids were like that. You couldn't wallow in your own misery when a tiny human needed your attention for their very survival.

Remy would do that for Wes. He'd be able to put one foot in front of the other because that four-year-old was a sweet handful. Not that I believed he was going to sink into a fit of depression without me, especially after only a few days.

Although he had looked gutted when I kissed him goodbye. Or maybe it was because his daughter was going to be ripped from him.

Me, on the other hand? I didn't know how I would go on living next door to the man I loved.

Yes, *loved*.

It seemed foolish to say that about someone I'd just met, but there was no way my heart could be breaking this badly if I wasn't madly in love with Wes.

I'd had a fling or two in the past. This wasn't it.

"Hi," I said to my mom, dropping the suitcase in the hallway. "I'm going to stay here until my roof gets fixed. Is that okay?"

"Well, of course, honey!" she replied brightly. "It would be great to have you here. But I thought you were staying with Wes?"

My mom scanned my face with interest when she turned to face me.

She was excited for me after meeting Wes and Remy. Hopeful, for the first time in ages.

I was about to dash her dreams.

She wouldn't be getting an adorable, red-headed step-grandchild, after all.

Maybe I wouldn't tell her just yet. I was liking this version of her, and I didn't want to be the reason for her to spiral down.

But her forehead creased in concern as she peered at me. "Something happened, didn't it? Did you have a fight? He seemed like such a good man. Respectful and all that."

My shoulders slumped, and tears burned behind my eyes again. I wasn't going to be able to keep it from her. I couldn't be cheerful for her tonight. I couldn't even keep it together for myself.

I sank into a kitchen chair in defeat, sighed, then sniffed. "Not a fight. But we broke up."

Her eyes widened. "Why would you break up if there wasn't a fight?"

"He and Remy's mom are involved in a custody battle, and it's going to be better for his chances of keeping Remy if I'm not in the picture."

Her mouth fell open in shock. "What? That's absurd.

Having you around just makes his home all the more stable! It's not like you're a felon or addict or something."

I dropped my head into my hands, my elbows resting on the table. "I don't want to talk about it, Mom."

I *couldn't* talk about it. Not without explaining the whole wolf thing, which was a secret I knew Wes–or anyone else in the pack–didn't want shared.

Mom sat down beside me and rubbed between my shoulder blades, like she had when I was a kid. "Sweetheart," her voice was soothing. "I'm so sorry. I could tell you really care about both of them. And I admit, I really liked them too. Remy's a... well, she reminds me a lot of you. Bright and intelligent. Busy, too."

Tears dripped into my hands even as I laughed. "I do like both of them," I said.

She cocked her head. "So, can you help me understand? Did Wes ask you to walk away?"

I shook my head. "No, but his ex doesn't want me around Remy. She made that very clear. I'm... I'm triggering to her, I guess. It just would be easier for them to sort things out if I wasn't part of the equation."

"But you *are* part of the equation." My mom's voice was soft, but firm, setting her hand on top of mine.

"Mom, you're not helping," I snapped then immediately regretted it.

My mom stood up and kissed the top of my head. I heard her moving around the kitchen, working on dinner.

"I'm sorry." I wiped my tears and stood to help her.

She put a hand out. "Sit down, sweetheart. I've got dinner covered."

"No, I'd rather be useful." I set the table and got us two glasses of ice water.

"You don't have to be strong all the time," my mom said after a moment, not looking my way.

It sounded like something Wes would say, which ripped a fresh hole in my chest.

"I know you took on too much responsibility as a young girl, after the divorce," she continued. "I had such a hard time functioning with the depression. You sacrificed your adolescence for me."

Wow. That was a heavy admission.

I was stunned by her words as I held the napkins. "No, Mom. We were in it together."

She turned from the counter to face me. "We shouldn't have been in it together. I was the grown up. I should have been there for you, and instead, it was the other way around."

My mom's words flayed me even more. God, why was she laying this on me right now? I was incapable of healing her wounds for her when I could barely stop the bleeding of my own.

"Joy...you sacrifice yourself for everyone else." She came over to me, took the napkins and set them on the table. Then she took my hand. "You spend your energy trying to make everyone happy. Cheering people up. Me, especially."

"So?" I croaked. I really didn't know why we were discussing my character flaws right now.

She gave my hand a squeeze. "So I want you to be selfish for a change."

"Mom, now is not the time to be selfish!" I stated firmly.

"I told you, I'm triggering to his ex. I need to take myself out of the situation."

"Well, that may be true," she said, her voice soft. "But I'm seeing my daughter in tears, which tells me that she's not happy with the choice she made. I'm just thinking sometimes when we think there's only two choices, it might be time to look for a third option. I know maybe I'm not the one to say that to you, that I need to say that to myself first. Huh?"

I let out a soft chuff of sad laughter.

"I... I did take your advice and told Clyde I was available for a drink this weekend." My mom gave me a shy and slightly embarrassed look then went back to the stove and finished cooking the stir-fry.

"What?" I lifted my head. "You did? That's great. He's been into you forever, and I'm glad you're finally giving him a chance. I'm so excited!"

She scooped the food into two bowls and set them on the table.

"I do like him, but I'm scared. I'm willing to try though."

We sat down, and I picked up my fork and moved the food around, but I was unable to eat. My stomach weighed two tons.

"What would it look like to fight for Wes?" my mom asked softly. I could tell she didn't want to talk more about her date with Clyde, and I didn't want to push it. One day at a time with her, even if she was in a streak of good days. So it was my love life–or lack of–that we returned to.

A rope knotted in my stomach. "I can't." My voice was full of misery. I felt the weight of a thousand pounds bearing down on my shoulders.

"You don't know how to make it work. But just keep asking questions. What other possibilities are available besides breaking up with him? You don't have to answer. I just want you to think about it. Think about a way where you can get what you want, too, for a change."

I let the tears drip down my face unchecked. Maybe my mom was right. I didn't know. But I did know that I appreciated my mom's attempt to help. It was nice to have her mother me for a change. To feel her love and caring. To have her be the one pulling me out of a slump. Or trying to.

"Thanks, Mom." I stood, leaving my dinner uneaten. "I'm going to go crawl under the covers and have a good cry."

Old me wouldn't have allowed herself even that luxury. But part of not self-sacrificing was letting myself feel my feelings.

And right now, all I felt was grief.

30

WES

I SLEPT FOR SHIT. My mate wasn't beside me, and my wolf was pissed. Impatient. Joy was right about one thing.

Remy came first. Always.

I had to take care of Soraya once and for all, and then I could drive over to Mrs. Wallace's place and get my mate back. Even if it meant tossing her over my fucking shoulder.

Dealing with my ex was the only way I was going to get Joy back. It was going to be tricky. I didn't know the council member she was bringing, and she had a strong case.

"It's going to be fine," Rob said when I absently refilled his mug of coffee.

He and Johnny had been here an hour, going over all the info Johnny had collected, and it was a lot. We were in the kitchen waiting. Me, impatiently. I didn't have a council member backing me in this matter, but a strong alpha and an enforcer on my side didn't hurt. Neither did the things we dug up since the day before.

"Telling you now, Alpha," I said. "If it's decided she gets Remy, I'm running."

Rob studied me, then nodded. I wasn't sure if it was because he agreed or if he nodded because he heard and understood.

Maybe he had more confidence in this little *get together* than I did. He didn't have a child being threatened.

Johnny, usually upbeat and smiling, sat quietly at the table. He was working on a laptop and busy typing. I went to refill his mug, but it was still full.

The doorbell rang.

I looked to Rob then Johnny.

This was it. Was I keeping my child or not?

31

WES

"Daddy, she's here." Remy ran into the kitchen. She didn't have a big smile on her face, like usual. In fact, she looked mulish and determined. If so much wasn't on the line, I'd panic about my child's mood because in ten years, she was going to be a handful.

I hadn't wanted to tell Remy anything about Soraya, but in case things went south this morning, I decided she needed to know what was going on.

I'd told her that Soraya was her biological mother, who wasn't very good at the job, but wanted another shot at it. I'd also told her I wasn't going to let that happen, if I could help it.

"Oh, yeah?" I said to Remy, trying to sound a shit-ton calmer than I really felt.

She nodded. Her hair was in two braids that I'd done. They were lopsided, but I doubted anyone noticed since she decided to pick out her own clothes to wear. Red shorts, a green and yellow striped top, and her pink rain boots. "Yeah. I can smell her." She crinkled her little nose. "She smells... dirty."

Johnny laughed outright. Rob's lips turned up, and I had to smile because she was so right.

"I think there's a spot for her on the council." Johnny came to his feet.

I hoisted Remy into my arms when the doorbell rang again.

"I guess we have to answer it," I muttered.

Rob nodded then followed me.

There on the stoop was Soraya. She was in a soft blue dress with wedge sandals that had ribbons tied around her ankles. Her outfit was fitting for a prayer revival.

Beside her was a man, mid-thirties. Dark hair. Dark gaze. Clean-shaven. He looked like he was from a big city pack based on his expensive clothes, expensive haircut and... did he have a manicure?

Fuck me.

Then I caught a whiff of his scent. It was mingled with Soraya's. Was that from them driving over here together? Or was she screwing him?

"There she is," Soraya cooed in an overly-bright fake voice. "Hello, Remington," Soraya said to Remy.

Remy turned her face away, wiggled in my arms to be put down, and ran off to her room.

I'd teach my child manners... with someone else.

I stepped back and let the duo inside.

I didn't offer them a seat.

Introductions were required, so I said, "This is Rob

Wolf, alpha of this region, and Johnny, our region's enforcer."

"I'm Tad Parker." He nodded to Rob first, then Johnny. "Council member of Soraya's home pack."

"We're not here to make friends. We're here for me to collect Remington," Soraya said. "I hope you've packed her things. We have a flight in a few hours and don't have time to linger."

"Hold up." Rob used a tinge of alpha command that registered in each of our bodies. It was authority that made you go still and listen. "I'd like to hear from the council member about his findings on this shift in parental rights." He crossed his arms over his chest, indicating he wasn't to be messed with.

We stood in my living room. I didn't offer anyone a chair. Or coffee. It was awkward and uncomfortable, but I wasn't going to make things easier or play nice.

Parker–because there was no way in hell I was going to call him *Tad*–cleared his throat. "Soraya brought it to my attention that her child is living with a human."

Both Soraya and Parker sniffed, then again.

I had no doubt the house still smelled like Joy. Even though I'd showered and put on fresh clothes since I saw her last, her scent lingered here in this room.

"There are no human/shifter pairs in your pack?" Rob asked.

"Other pairs are not in question right now," Tad added.

"I have many mated, mixed pairs in our pack. Even with children. There is no pack law or even a consensus that this is not accepted."

"I don't mean to disrespect your pack, Alpha, but Soraya wants what's best for her child."

"The disrespect was definitely received, Parker." Warning laced Rob's voice. "Watch it. Wes found and marked his fated mate."

Soraya's surprised gaze flicked to me.

That's right. Joy wasn't some rando human I had sleeping over. She was my one true mate. The female nature intended for me.

"The union is solid," Rob went on. "Permanent. Nothing can come between what has been fated."

While Parker might be a council member, he was no alpha.

"Tad has given his judgment that Remington should be with me, her mother, free from any *contamination*."

"Documentation?" Johnny held out his hand.

Parker sighed, reached into his pocket, and handed him a piece of paper.

Johnny read it then passed it to Rob.

After a thorough review, Rob passed it back. I didn't need to see it if they had.

"It's interesting, Parker, why Soraya is so interested in her daughter now, after no contact since three weeks after her birth."

"I want to know that, too." I crossed my arms over my chest mimicking Rob.

"There is no statute of limitations on being a good mother," Soraya said.

"No, there isn't," I agreed, giving her a pointed look.

"See, he agrees." Parker pointed my way.

"I agreed on her statement," I snapped. "Her statement

doesn't indicate that she, personally, is in fact, a good mother."

Soraya's green eyes narrowed, and she looked murderous. "She's coming with me. You can't stop me. If you try, there's a council member, an alpha, and an enforcer here to witness to what we can all agree is against pack rules."

"Not this pack," Rob growled. "And you're in my pack territory."

"I am a *council* member," Parker snapped back. Council members comprised shifters' governing law. They were the judges of our kind. They outranked alphas.

"Your council doesn't rule this territory," Rob continued.

"I had a feeling you'd pull this kind of bullshit," Soraya huffed.

It was my turn to narrow my gaze at how she had me cornered. I hated this woman. I wanted to wish I'd never laid eyes upon her, let alone fucked her, but she gave me Remy, and for that, I wouldn't change a thing.

"That's why I stopped at the sheriff's office before I came," Soraya bit out. "The *human* law enforcement. I filed kidnapping charges on you for taking my daughter. They should be here any minute to arrest you and ensure I get custody."

JOY

I FELT NO BETTER today than I had after crying myself to sleep last night, but I wasn't my mother.

I wasn't going to stay in bed with my covers over my head for days at a time.

So I dragged myself out of bed at Mom's and went to my studio to work on a replacement platter for the shipment that had broken.

There was a strange truck and car parked in front of Wes' house.

Soraya would be over there now, arguing her right to take Remy.

God, it took everything in my power not to run over there and back him up. To tell her what a wonderful father Wes was. How much he cared for Remy. How she was his entire world.

But I would only make things worse. I would only hurt

his case.

So I perched on my stool at my painting table. A paintbrush was in one hand, the once-baked platter in the other. It was time to get it glazed, along with the few other pieces that were ready, before I gave them the final fire in the kiln.

"Joy!"

I spun around at Remy's little voice.

She ran to me and wrapped herself around my legs in an awkward hug. I set my things down and hugged her back. My chest constricted like a tight band was wrapped around my ribs.

"What are you doing here?" I asked her.

It had only been a day, but I missed her.

"Does your dad know you're over here?"

She shook her head against my thighs. I picked her up and plopped her on the table. One of her rain boots fell off and dropped to the concrete floor.

"Sweetie, you aren't allowed to be here without your dad's permission. Remember how scared he was last time?"

"That smelly lady is here," she said, cutting me off.

Right. I looked up but couldn't see through the garage wall to Wes' house. Were they trying to take Remy? Was she over here hiding?

"Soraya?" I didn't know if Wes had told her that she was her mother.

Remy's eyes filled with tears. "Her. She says I have to go with her. You have to come and tell them you're my real mommy, and I don't need her."

Oh boy. Instantly, tears sprung to my eyes. "That's not how it works, sweetie. She is your mommy."

Remy shook her head, and her eyes filled with tears. "SHE IS NOT!" she shouted. "I WON'T GO WITH HER!"

I didn't blame her one bit. If there was a moment for a tantrum, this was it.

"Your daddy is making it right. Don't you worry."

He'd prove to Soraya that he and I weren't together. How, I had no idea, but he'd do it. He was that good of a father and protector.

"I want to stay here with you," she cried.

I shook my head. "Nope. Your dad is going to put you in time out for running off again. Plus, we need to get you back before he worries."

I'd take her to her back deck and make sure she went inside. I didn't dare have a four-year-old walk back to her house, even if it was only thirty feet door to door, by herself. Plus, Remy had a very bad–and dangerous–habit of running off. I didn't trust her not to run because she was so upset and could get hurt.

I scooped her up, set her on her feet, got the boot back on, and took her hand. "Come on, before your dad worries."

What I did for this kid. God, I didn't want to see Wes again. I definitely didn't want to mess things up for him. Seeing Remy was hard enough. And giving her back? Heart breaking. But Wes really was going to panic when he couldn't find her. He had enough to worry about right now. I could, at least, get her back safe. One less thing on his big, broad, sexy shoulders.

As I stepped up on the back porch with Remy, I could hear the deep voices of Wes and maybe Rob Wolf, as well as the nasty bite of Soraya's voice.

"...mate or not, she's human. I don't want my child raised in a mixed home."

The knot in my stomach tightened to epic proportions.

Please let Wes win this battle.

"Go inside," I whispered to Remy.

But the child refused to let go of my hand, bursting into tears and wrapping her little arms around my leg.

Eek. I didn't want to interrupt their meeting.

"The council does not like to separate children from their parents," a man said. "Wes, perhaps you could return to–"

"I'm not leaving my mate," Wes exploded.

"See?" Remy turned her blotchy face up to mine.

My nose grew hot.

"Joy is human, that's true. She's human, and she's perfect. She's brighter than the sun, bringing happiness and love to everyone she touches."

My throat constricted.

It sounded like Wes was choked up, too. "She's perfect for me, and she's perfect for Remy. She *cares* about Remy. She cares so much she was willing to walk away from us since you insisted, so I could keep my little girl."

Tears filled my eyes.

"No!" Remy dashed forward and threw open the back door. "This is my *real* mom," she declared loudly to the room, sweeping her arm toward me before I could disappear. "And you can't make her leave!"

33

WES

JOY. She was here.

Fuck me, my mate was here.

My wolf howled with, well, joy.

I walked swiftly forward to scoop Remy up, then went to Joy and pulled her into me. I kissed her forehead, in front of her messy bun. She smelled like sunshine and my mate.

"I'm sorry," she began. "I didn't mean to inter–"

"No. No one's going to make Joy leave," I said, cutting her off. She had *nothing* to apologize for. "And *no one* is taking Remy from us." I put alpha command into my voice.

Joy didn't feel it, but a shudder ran through Remy's body, and Soraya froze. "We'll see what the cops have to say about that," she said, when she'd recovered.

"This is a waste of my time," Rob said to Parker. "My enforcer has some data of our own to share, if the council member will listen."

The look Rob gave him said he didn't have a choice. He really didn't, actually. Council members heard both sides of a problem.

"Very well," Parker conceded.

Soraya huffed and tapped her foot on the floor.

Johnny stepped forward. "I offer you my condolences, Soraya, on last week's death of your father."

Parker's head whipped to Soraya.

"I should also offer you condolences on the fact that you didn't receive a dime of his vast fortune as owner of Stanton Oil. The will states that his granddaughter, Remington Sparks, is Martin Stanton's sole beneficiary."

Johnny had dug up this information since I called him yesterday. His network of enforcer connections came through. Thank fuck.

This was the real reason Soraya had suddenly shown up to claim Remy. She wanted to get her hands on that money. When we learned that detail yesterday, I was equally relieved and fucking furious. The conniving, heartless bitch.

"Is this true?" Parker asked Soraya.

If looks could kill, we'd all be dead with the fierceness of Soraya's glare. "Yes," she pretty much snarled. "So?"

"It's interesting, Parker, that a mother who has had zero interest in her child until that child becomes a billionaire."

34

JOY

Billionaire? Holy shit.

That made so much sense. God, I felt bad that the man had died, but giving everything to Remy? He must have loved her or hated his daughter. Maybe both.

Johnny ran a hand over the back of his neck. "I also collected some stories about how the two of you are, shall we say, shacking up? I think we can all say we smell her on you."

My eyes bugged out of my head. Soraya and, based on his clothes and appearance, the fake outdoorsman, were an item? I couldn't smell anything, but I was only *human*.

That guy shifted uncomfortably, and Soraya pursed her lips and made a very unattractive face.

Then she stomped over to me, poked me in the chest. "You. You don't get to enjoy my inheritance! I'll end you before that happens."

My eyes widened in surprise.

Wes pulled me away from Soraya and halfway behind him. As if she'd have to get through him to get to me. "My mate has *nothing* to do with your conniving, scheming ways."

"Parker, I've never laid eyes on this woman before," Rob began, talking about Soraya, "but I'm going to give you some advice. You're going to want to cut ties with her right now. If your document was based on her giving good head, then your role on the council isn't the only thing you need to worry about."

The guy, Parker, blanched and looked to Soraya as if determining whether the BJ really was worth it.

"Yes, Alpha," he said, then tucked tail and... ran. Right out the door.

Holy shit.

I could guess what an alpha was. Rob did radiate quiet authority. Power. But every time I met Rob Wolf, he was so chill. Of course, none of his alpha-ness had been directed my way. But seeing that guy cower and literally flee...

Impressive.

Soraya wasn't as smart. She remained, her hands on her hips, and she somehow managed to both smirk and glare at the same time.

There was a knock on the still-open door.

Soraya smiled. "Good, the sheriff's here. Now this will all be resolved."

35

WES

FOR THE FIRST time in over twenty-four hours, I could breathe again.

My mate was beside me. The council member had left.

Now we just had the sheriff to deal with, and with any luck–

In walked the deputy sheriff, Kyle Abbott, followed by the sheriff of Cooper Valley, Levi, who happened to be a shifter, packmate, and friend.

I took great satisfaction in watching Soraya's self-satisfied little smile droop when she caught a whiff of Levi.

That's right, bitch. The Sheriff of Cooper Valley is a wolf.

Joy didn't know that, though, and she stepped forward, and held out her hand to halt them. "Sheriff, Deputy, I don't know what this woman told you, but it's all lies."

Levi took off his hat and studied Joy. "I'm aware."

Soraya's jaw went slack at his words.

Kyle Abbott, the deputy sheriff, was a human, but his daughter, Riley, was mated to Cody, one of our packmates. He knew and kept our shifter secret.

Whatever tale Soraya had spun must've been to Kyle because she wouldn't have known he was a wolf. She'd wanted to pit a human on this but chose the wrong one. Clearly, Kyle went to Clint with the complaint, and they put it together.

Because they hadn't bought a word of it. Thank fuck.

Kyle looked at Soraya. "Ma'am, did you know it's a crime to file a false police report?"

I smelled desperation on Soraya. She stabbed a finger in my direction. "He kidnapped my daughter from me when she was a baby. I just now found her, and I demand that you arrest him!" Her voice was shrill.

Kyle Abbott propped a shoulder against my door frame in a casual stance. "Remind me," he drawled slowly, "What is the penalty for filing a false report with a peace officer in Montana again, Sheriff?"

"Up to six months in prison in the county jail," Levi answered.

Soraya's upper lip curled. "A prison wouldn't hold me."

"Nah, it probably wouldn't," Johnny interjected. "That's where I come in." He took a menacing step toward her. "As *enforcer.*"

Shifter enforcers carried out the sentences of the council. Because human prisons couldn't hold our kind, those sentences were usually capital punishment. Johnny may be young, but he'd seen more death than I had, even working the rodeo.

That threat did the trick. Soraya shot toward the door, bumping into Kyle.

"My suggestion to you," I said, glancing at Remy's sweet face. "Is that you stop traumatizing your daughter by threatening to take her from her loving family." I glanced at Joy to make sure she was on board. That we were a family–the three of us.

As always, those perfect lips of hers tipped up in a smile.

"If you ever hope she'll find it in her heart to give you a distribution from her inheritance," I added.

A carrot and a stick.

Soraya's nervous glance went from Remy's face to mine then to Johnny's. "Remy, Mommy loves you," she said.

"Oh, please," Joy muttered with an eye roll.

Remy reached for Joy, and I transferred her over to my mate. "This is my mommy."

"I know." Soraya had taken my suggestion. "But I'm your other mommy. And I love you very much."

"Okay, byeeee," Joy cut in.

Soraya flicked a glance at Kyle, and he took his time moving out of the threshold of the door, so she could get through.

"Mommy will come and visit you all the time, okay, baby?"

"Byeeeee," Remy mimicked Joy's dismissal.

Levi and Rob chuckled. It was probably not the best thing for her to have learned, but like most everything a four-year-old did, it was damn cute.

Soraya went out the door, and Kyle shut it behind her. "Byeeee," he said. "I think that's the last we'll see of her."

Rob nodded, offering a smile. "I agree."

Remy giggled.

So did Joy.

Then, unbelievably, I found myself laughing, too.

It was over.

Remy was still here. So was Joy.

All the crushing despair of the last day disappeared. Even the longer-term, familiar weight and solitude of carrying this two-person family on my own for the past four years lifted away.

I had everything I could ever want.

My life was complete.

36

JOY

WES PULLED my wrists together and tied them to the headboard with a wide, pink ribbon. I'm not sure where it came from, but I suspected it was one of Remy's hair ribbons.

She was asleep, and I was now naked.

Wes' eyes glowed green. Hunger was etched in every line of his face, but he killed me by saying, "I'm going to take a shower, and you're going to wait here and think about what a bad girl you were."

My mouth fell open, and I tugged at my wrists. It was a *ribbon,* and I could get out if I tried hard enough. I didn't want to.

"Bad girl?" I protested.

He'd spent the day telling me how amazing I was. How much it meant to him that I'd shown up to have his back and also how much it meant that I was willing to sacrifice my own desires and happiness for his. We'd spent the entire day holding each other, all three of us.

Now I was a *bad girl*?

"I don't think so," I told him.

A smirk curved his lips. He was smiling more often now. I could definitely get used to it.

"Bad girl. You broke my fucking heart yesterday when you walked out. And I want to be sure you've faced the consequences, so it doesn't happen again."

The sexy way he said *consequences* let me know it was a very sexy punishment he had in mind.

The spanky kind, I imagined.

I wriggled my hips impatiently. I needed him to touch me now.

But the big jerk sauntered sexily off to the en suite bathroom.

I stared at the ceiling and huffed. As the feelings of ridiculousness set in–I was tied by a ribbon bare assed naked to a bed without any kind of sexy fun happening–the shower shut off. Wes came out and stood before the bed as he dried himself.

Holy hell, droplets of water worked their way down his body, and they were swiped up. I followed his hand and the small strawberry towel–the same one from when we first met–as it roamed his perfect torso.

This time, his dick was hard. Big. Long. Thick. For me.

"How'd it feel to have me walk away?" he asked, rubbing the towel over his wet head.

My mouth fell open. Then closed. Then open.

"You... you went to the shower, so I'd know what it was like when someone left?"

He shrugged a shoulder. "I wanted you in there with me."

I tugged at the ribbon. "Whose fault is that?" I snapped. I wasn't happy any longer. "Wes, let me up."

He sensed that things had changed and leaned over and tugged at the knot. The second I was free, I popped up onto my knees, so we were eye to eye. Me on the bed, him standing before it.

Both naked. It was time to bare even more.

"I'm sorry if I hurt you, but I won't ever come between you and Remy. Ever."

He growled. "I know. I love you all the more for it."

Tears filled my eyes. He reached out and swiped one that slipped down my cheek.

"We were never apart. You didn't know it, but I never considered you gone. You were correct, I had to take care of Remy first, but then I was coming after you."

My eyes widened. "You were?"

"You're mine. My mate. My partner. My soul."

"Wes," I breathed. Okay, I was happy again. I put my fingers to the spot on my breast where he bit me. No, *marked*. There was a hint of a scab but it didn't hurt. "Is it because of this?"

"Yes."

"Because it forced you to return?"

He frowned. "No. Because that mark means we are permanent. Nothing will separate us. Nothing will break what we've chosen to join."

"Oh. I love you, too. I wanted the mark for those reasons."

"Now will you fucking kiss me?" he asked.

I couldn't help but smile, then grin outright. "Now you can spank me for being a bad girl." I turned around and dropped to my hands and knees. Glancing over my shoulder, I looked to Wes. "I'm ready to face the consequences."

37

WES

Joy loved me bossy, so I let my dominant side out. I was ready to show it to her again.

I grabbed one of the pillows and dropped it in the center of the bed.

"Lie over this. I want that pretty ass of yours in the air."

Joy complied, wiggling her hips.

"Fuck, that's gorgeous." I slapped one cheek, then watched my handprint bloom on her pale skin. My dick was so fucking hard from the sight. "You're so beautiful."

I tugged her wrists behind her back and used the ribbon to tie them together there. "Are you ready for your spanking?"

"Yes, sir."

I chuckled—still a foreign experience in my chest. But it was happening more often now. Joy had walked into my life and turned on the lights. I hadn't realized I'd been trying to function in the dark all this time. That I could live the same life, walk the same steps, but be five hundred times happier than I was before. I didn't know this could even be possible.

"*Sir*...I like that," I rumbled. I slapped her other ass cheek a little harder.

She yelped but then looked over her shoulder as best she could with her arms bound behind her back. "Thank you, sir, may I have another?" Her expression was coquettish. I loved that she was uninhibited with me, that she didn't hide any part of herself.

Even more of a laugh tumbled from my lips this time. She was unbearably cute. She made my chest fill with so much warmth, I felt it would burst.

"Good girl." I gave her another spank.

"I thought I was a bad girl," she sassed, wiggling her hips.

"Oh, now you're asking for it." I delivered a flurry of spanks on her upturned ass, concentrating in the lower portion where she sat. She wiggled over the pillow as she squeaked and moaned. The scent of her arousal made my dick stand out hard and straight.

I paused and said, "I'm going to fuck that gorgeous ass tonight and show you who's really boss."

I waited to see how she took that news. I obviously would never do anything she wasn't comfortable with.

She moaned.

"I want every part of you." I leaned over her, nipped her ear. "Will you give yourself to me in every way?"

"Wes, oh, yes." I'd take that as consent in this scenario.

"Good girl." I couldn't help but say it again.

I slid my fingers between her legs and rubbed her glorious honey up and around her clit.

She spread her legs wider for more.

Instead, I spanked her some more, turning her ass a sexy shade of pink. She gasped and moaned. I could tell it was getting too intense when she started listing away from my hand, and I stopped to rub away the sting.

"Good girl." I rewarded her with my fingers between her legs again. "You're always a good girl, even when you're my bad girl," I told her. Because this definitely wasn't real punishment. This was pleasure for both of us.

She was my mate, whom I had a deep biological need to satisfy, and my mate liked it when I bossed her around.

I hooked my thumbs on the insides of her thighs and spread them wide, pushing her reddened cheeks open to get my tongue between her legs.

She cried out, jerking in pleasure at the first touch of my tongue. I tortured her with it, delving between her labia, penetrating her with the tip.

My cock throbbed, aching to be inside her. I knelt behind Joy and rubbed the blunt head of my dick through her juices, nudging gently at her entrance. She was so wet and welcoming, I slid right in. Fuck, she felt good. Tight. Wet. Hot.

My groan mingled with her soft moan of pleasure. I tugged her hips up, so she was up on her knees, and then I moved the pillow under her chest. Her wrists were still tied behind her back, and I slid my palms down the sides of her body and back to her hips to grip them.

"Mmm." The sensation of sliding in and out of her channel sent me to another galaxy. I kept it slow, savoring the way she squeezed around my cock when I went deep. The catch of her breath. The shivers in her legs.

"Mmm," she moaned back at me. We were in perfect sync. Me giving. Her receiving. Or was it really the other way around–she gave her gorgeous body to me, and I received it? It was a perfect harmony loop as far as I was concerned. Our bodies engaged in an act of love. An embodiment of fate.

Every time we came together like this, it got better.

I wasn't going to let her come. Not yet. We had other things to explore tonight. We'd been frantic in the past, our lust hazing everything. Now, we had all the time in the world.

I slowed my strokes, making them a tease.

She pushed her hips back, trying to encourage me to move deeper. "Wes," she moaned.

I slid out.

She whimpered.

I gave her ass a slap. "Stay right there, honey."

"You'd better not be taking another shower," she teased.

I chuckled. Damn. Third time. This female was going to give me a personality change.

I grabbed a bottle of lube I had picked up this afternoon for tonight's festivities and uncapped it. "Little chilly here," I warned.

Returning to the bed, I pulled her ass cheeks apart and dropped a dollop of lube between them.

"Ooh!" Her anus squeezed in response to the sudden sensation.

"Have you taken anyone back here before?" I rubbed

my thumb over her back entrance, massaging the lube in. I wasn't sure if I wanted to know the answer.

"No."

Thank fuck. Yes, it was wrong of me to be so possessive of this part of her, to take something that belonged to only me, but I was a fucking wolf.

To a human, I was alpha to the core.

I applied a little pressure, breaching her hole and stretching it to take my thumb. Slowly, carefully, I worked. "Are you nervous?"

A shiver went through her. "A little."

"I'm gonna take good care of you, honey. I'll make it good. Do you trust me?" I withdrew my thumb and massaged her ass, squeezing and rubbing it. Felt the heat of those lush globes against my palms.

"Yes."

"Good girl." I untied her wrists and leaned over to kiss her mouth, plunging my tongue in deep.

She moaned against my lips.

I rearranged her hips back down on the pillows because being lower was an easier position for anal. The flesh wasn't stretched too tight the way it would be if I'd left her on her knees, and I wanted this first time to be as easy on her as possible.

"Put your fingers between your legs, honey. I want you to touch yourself while I'm fucking your ass."

Joy complied, lifting her hips to slide her hand underneath her as I lubed my cock up. Watching her was a sight. Another time, I'd sit in my reading chair and watch her touch herself and make herself come in our bed.

I spread her cheeks to get at her back entrance. I nudged her with the head of my cock.

Instinctively, she tightened.

I waited. "Relax, honey," I murmured. "This is gonna feel good."

Her right rosebud softened as she exhaled.

"Take a deep breath and then push back at me."

She obeyed, and I gained entrance with a silent pop.

"Oh!" she called out. At first, I stilled, letting her adjust. It was so fucking tight already, I could come just like this.

When her body relaxed even more, I went slowly, letting the tight ring of muscles slide open without me insisting. Without creating any tension or resistance. "That's it, honey. A little further, and we'll be past the head, and then you're going to love the way it feels."

She braced, so I stilled.

Sweat dotted my brow, and I intentionally kept my fingers relaxed on her hips. "You control it, baby. Push back when you're ready."

She did just that, and the thickest part of my cock slipped all the way in.

Holy fucking shit. "Feel good?" I asked through gritted teeth.

She moaned. I heard the slick of her fingers playing with her pussy.

"Good girl. You keep working that juicy pussy of yours while I work your ass," I told her.

"Y–es, sir."

Fuck, she was cute. Even though I'd already marked her as mine, I wanted to devour her. Consume her. She was incredible.

I moved slowly inside her, keeping my strokes even and straight. As I continued, her moans grew louder. Her back arched deeper.

"Please, Wes," she moaned.

"Please, what, honey?" I thought she wanted more by the wanton tone of her voice, but I needed to be sure.

"I need to come."

"Okay, honey. I'm gonna fuck you a little faster, but I'll still be careful with you, okay?"

"Yes." I loved the needy whine in her voice.

I picked up my speed, allowing my pleasure to rush to the fore. My balls drew up. I lowered my hips down to meet hers, so I wouldn't pump too erratically or hard. I reached my fingers under her hips to tangle with hers between her legs.

She was sopping wet, her pussy so plump and open that two of my fingers sank immediately in.

"Yes, yes!" she cried out.

I humped her ass, pressing the heel of my hand against her clit and wiggling my fingers inside her pussy.

"God, yes! Please, Wes! Please!"

My eyes rolled back in my head. I knew they were glowing. My wolf couldn't get enough of our mate. I allowed myself to topple over the brink of control. I plunged deep into her ass and came.

"Come for me, honey," I growled. I used my fingers between her legs.

Her body quivered. Sweat coated her skin. She was hot to the touch.

She shrieked as she came, her pussy squeezing around

my fingers, which she urged deeper with hers. Our hips bucked together as one unit.

Fireworks burst behind my eyes. Joy's scent surrounded me. I bit her shoulder–not a mating bite–not enough to break the skin–but out of a need to have all of her, in every way.

I would always be ravenous for my mate this way. It would never stop.

When our pleasure had been thoroughly wrung out and we'd caught our breaths, I eased out of her.

"Stay right there, baby. I'll be back," I murmured against her nape.

"Mmmm," she moaned.

I went to the bathroom to wash my hands and get a wet, warm washcloth, then returned to clean my mate. She was soft and pliant, wilted with her eyes closed. A smile tipped up the corner of her lips.

I tossed the cloth on the floor and rolled us to our sides, pulling the pillow out from under her hips.

I pulled a sheet over us and curled my larger body around hers. "Mine," I murmured in her ear. She was softly pressed against me.

"Yes," she murmured, leaning her head down to kiss my forearm. "I'm yours."

"I also love you." I kissed and nibbled her shoulder. "Wolves mate instinctively. I knew you were mine by scent, but all the human emotions are there, too, Joy. I want you to know that."

She turned in my arms to face me. Her blue eyes met mine. They were sated and satisfied, but I couldn't miss her happiness. "I love you, too, Wes."

I kissed her tenderly this time, cradling her cheek in my hand. "I can't believe I get to spend the rest of my life with you."

She kissed me back. "Ditto." Then tears welled in her eyes. "I can't believe I'm a mom!"

I went still. We hadn't talked about her taking on Remy, too. "Is it okay? Too much? We can go slowly."

She shook her head, her messy hair sliding against my skin. "No, I'm all in. Remy is mine. She seemed to know it from the start, too."

I thought about that for a moment, realized she picked up on something wolf-ish before I did. "You're right." I remembered with awe. "She did say you smelled good the first time she met you. Then she said she knew you were human, but you were the good kind."

Definitely the good kind.

"We were meant to be," Joy said softly. "You, me, and Remy."

"Always and forever."

"You are my forever," she said, which made me feel taller than a mountain. I pulled her closer, so she could lay her head on my shoulder and curl into me to fall asleep.

"You're incredible."

38

JOY

"I THINK SHE WANTS CHAPERONES," I told Wes as we drove toward my mother's house.

It was four days after the Soraya showdown, and things had settled into a routine. A routine of being a family of three. Busy with Remy and my pottery during the day, nights spent in bed with Wes having sex. Talking. Learning about each other.

Remy didn't mention her mother. Not once. All she knew was that she was gone, and that seemed to be enough.

"If this guy isn't good for her, be prepared for me to kick him out," Wes muttered, eyes on the road.

My lips twitched at how protective he was of Mom. She'd called the day before and asked us over for dinner. Dinner with *Clyde*. It seemed their date had gone well, and this was their second date.

With us and a four-year-old tagging along.

I thought it was cute. I'd known Clyde for a long time, unlike Wes, and wasn't concerned he was going to mess with my mom's emotions. He really did like her.

No man doggedly asked a woman out for years if he wasn't truly interested.

"Just wait ten years," I said.

He glanced at me and frowned. I thumbed over my shoulder to the back seat where Remy was humming to herself.

Wes downright growled now, catching on. "Fourteen? Not happening. She can date when she's twenty."

"What about full moon ru–"

His surprise braking and pulling the car over cut off my words.

I looked around. "What's the matter? Did we hit something?"

He turned in his seat and set his forearm on the steering wheel. "Are you trying to have more *consequences?*"

I gulped, remembering it took two days for my butt to stop hurting after the last time, and that had been in fun.

"My *quences* weren't fun," Remy grumbled from the back seat. "I had to work at the ranch for the time everyone went lookin' for me. I don't like moving rocks."

"You're not supposed to," Wes said.

I bit my lip. Wes decided Remy needed to be punished for her running off, even though the reasons were solid. She needed to know how dangerous her actions were. So he'd taken her to the ranch with him the other morning and made her move river rocks–softball-sized ones that weren't too heavy–and put them in a pile by a nearby cottonwood tree. Then she had to move them back. Marina helped her for a little while. Then Johnny. It hadn't been forced labor by any stretch, but to a little girl, it had seemed huge. It had been necessary.

It took her thirty minutes, but Wes told her that was the amount of everyone's time she'd wasted when she'd gone off on her moon run. She owed them that time helping out.

"I'm not going to run off any longer," she added, in case Wes was planning to add any more rock shuffling to her day.

"Good. Then you can tell Mrs. Wallace that you can have an extra cherry in your juice."

"Yay! What're we waitin' for then?" she asked.

"Yeah, what are we waiting for?" I repeated, trying to look sweet and innocent.

I wondered that, too. Wes stared at both of us, then rolled his eyes. "Women."

Before Wes could put the car back in gear, his cell rang. It came through the dashboard.

"Afternoon, Wes. Levi here."

For a moment, I freaked, thinking he was going to say that Soraya was back. I grabbed Wes' hand.

"I'm in the truck with my girls," Wes said, most likely warning the sheriff that there was a four-year-old with big ears. Especially big, since shifters supposedly heard really well.

"I won't keep you. Just wanted to tell you that I worked with Selena Jenkins. Papers were drawn up as you wanted."

Selena Jenkins was a lawyer, but also a shifter, who Levi said had helped their pack members in the past. The papers offered Soraya a sum of money in exchange for relinquishing any custody rights to Remy. Wes would have full custody. Permanently. The sum was vast for a not-quite-starving artist like me, but not for a billionaire.

I had a feeling he'd have paid anything to make Soraya go away and never come back.

"And?"

"And they're all signed," Levi replied. "Congratulations."

Wes sighed, then smiled. "Thanks."

It was over. Soraya was gone. She'd gotten what she wanted–money. Wes got a guarantee that she could never take Remy away.

The call ended, and he pulled back on the road.

"That was a good use of the money," I told him. When all of a sudden one had enough money to buy a fleet of planes, it was hard to even know where to start spending it. Which Wes didn't seem to want to do. He was content. Remy was happy.

That was all that mattered.

He nodded. "Another good use is getting your house fixed. I'm not waiting for the insurance to go through."

My mouth opened. "What? I–I can pay you back."

"Do you want me to pull the truck over again?" he warned.

"No!" Remy called.

"Wes–"

"We're a family now, honey. I don't plan on buying a yacht and putting your name on it or anything, but I think we can swing fixing your roof."

He had a point.

"Okay," I agreed. "I didn't really want a second job at Cody's."

"The list of consequences is getting longer the more you talk," he said, his voice tipped quiet.

"You don't want to move rocks!" Remy said from the back, proving she could hear anyway.

We pulled into Mom's driveway, and Wes put the truck in park.

"Can I go ask for extra cherries now?" Remy asked.

"Yes," Wes said.

She undid the buckles on the car seat herself and climbed out. She raced off to the house, leaving her door wide open.

"You're not getting a job at Cody's. I can support you."

I turned to face him fully. "I'm not going to sit around eating cherries all day, Wes."

"I know that. I want you to focus on your passion. Your pottery."

I cocked my head. "Really?"

"Of course."

I swallowed, looked down at our joined hands. "I was thinking about turning my house into a shop. Maybe a co-op for other artists to show and sell their work." I looked up through my lashes at Wes, unsure if the idea was a good one. "I mean, since I'm not living there any longer."

Reaching out, he unclipped my seat belt and pulled me across the center console.

"Wes!" I cried.

Once I was settled–a little awkwardly–in his lap, he kissed me.

And kissed me.

If we weren't in Mom's driveway, we'd take things a lot further. Heck, all the way.

"Miz Wall said to stop kissin' and come inside!" Remy called from the front stoop.

I looked to Wes, and we laughed.

"Can you make a baby brother first? Cassie at school says her parents made a baby 'cause they kissed all the time."

My eyes widened, and then I laughed some more. Wes' eyes narrowed and heated.

We hadn't talked about a baby.

But–

Maybe?

For now, I was happy. I was loved. I was a mother. Life was perfect.

And crazy. Because a certain four-year-old was definitely going to run us ragged.

———

Ready for more Wolf Ranch?
Read Dangerous now!

Pack Rule #10 – Keep control of your inner wolf.
I live alone on the mountain for a reason.
I'm dangerous—too strong, too aggressive, too close to feral.
But then *she* shows up—with sweet curves, sultry voice, and a scent that drives my wolf insane.
A gorgeous human, pouring drinks at Cody's Saloon and hiding a shattered past behind her smile.

I know the second I scent her—she's mine. My mate. The one I was made for.

My wolf surges to claim her. But she's just escaped a controlling ex who tried to silence her music, her voice, her very soul. My alpha instincts are everything she fears–I'm possessive. Dominant. Overwhelming. And she's terrified of losing her freedom again.

I've held back my entire life. From the pack. From power. From the madness in my blood.

But I won't hold back from her. Not when she's what anchors me.

I'll protect her. Please her. Put her music back in the world. And if she'll let me, I'll make her mine—completely. Even if I have to unleash every dark, dangerous part of myself to do it.

NOTE FROM VANESSA & RENEE

Guess what? We've got some bonus content for you with Joy and Wes. Yup, there's more!

Click here to read more!
or go to this link:
https://vanessavaleauthor.com/v/2k9

GET A FREE VANESSA VALE BOOK!

Join my mailing list to be the first to know of new releases, free books, special prices and other author giveaways.

http://freeromanceread.com

WANT FREE RENEE ROSE BOOKS?

Receive a slew of free Renee Rose books: Go to http://sub scribepage.com/alphastemp to sign up for Renee Rose's newsletter and receive free books. In addition to the free stories and bonus material, you will also get special pricing, exclusive previews and news of new releases.

Did you know you can buy direct from Renee Rose? Get signed books, special editions, and heavily discounted bundles. Use this coupon for an additional 10% discount on your entire order - **READER10** or go here https://shop.reneeroseromance.com/discount/READER10

ALSO BY RENEE ROSE

Alpha King

Alpha Varsity

Bad Boy Alphas Series

Alpha's Temptation

Alpha's Danger

Alpha's Prize

Alpha's Challenge

Alpha's Obsession

Alpha's Desire

Alpha's War

Alpha's Mission

Alpha's Bane

Alpha's Secret

Alpha's Prey

Alpha's Sun

Shifter Ops

Alpha's Moon

Alpha's Vow

Alpha's Revenge

Alpha's Fire

Alpha's Rescue

Alpha's Command

Werewolves of Wall Street

Big Bad Boss: Midnight

Big Bad Boss: Moon Mad

Big Bad Boss: Marked

Big Bad Boss: Mated

Big Bad Bully

Bad Boy Bears Series

Alpha's Claim

Alpha's Mate

Solo Paranormal Romance

Claimed by the Storm

Alpha Doms Series

Dominion (complete collection)

The Alpha's Hunger

The Alpha's Promise

The Alpha's Punishment

The Alpha's Protection

Contemporary

Chicago Bratva

"Prelude" in Black Light: Roulette War

The Director

The Fixer

"Owned" in Black Light: Roulette Rematch

The Enforcer

The Soldier

Alpha Mountain

Hero

Rebel

Warrior

Master Me Series

Her Royal Master

Her Russian Master

Her Marine Master

Yes, Doctor

Her Russian Master

Her Marine Master

Her Fire Master

Her Hollywood Master

Her Stepbrother Master

Double Doms Series

Theirs to Punish

Theirs to Protect

Holiday Feel-Good

Scoring with Santa

Saved

Other Contemporary

Black Light: Valentine Roulette

Black Light: Roulette Redux

Black Light: Celebrity Roulette

Black Light: Roulette War

Black Light: Roulette Rematch

Punishing Portia (written as Darling Adams)

The Professor's Girl

Safe in his Arms

Sci-Fi

Zandian Masters Series

His Human Slave

His Human Prisoner

Training His Human

His Human Rebel

His Human Vessel

His Mate and Master

Zandian Pet

Their Zandian Mate

His Human Possession

Zandian Brides

Night of the Zandians

Bought by the Zandians

Mastered by the Zandians

Zandian Lights

Kept by the Zandian

Claimed by the Zandian

ALSO BY VANESSA VALE

For the most up-to-date listing of my books:

vanessavalebooks.com

Cowboys of Devil's Ditch

Trig

Colt

Bray

Beau

Cam

Zeb

Shep

Buck

Hayes

The Hitman and the Fixer

Hannah and the Hitman

Fiona and the Fixer

On A Manhunt

Manhunt

Man Candy

Man Cave

Man Sprain

Man Scape

Man Handle

Man Spread

Alpha Mountain

Hero

Rebel

Warrior

Billionaire Ranch

North

South

East

West

Bachelor Auction

Teach Me The Ropes

Hand Me The Reins

Back In The Saddle

Wolf Ranch

Rough

Wild

Feral

Savage

Fierce

Ruthless

Primal

Rugged

Ravenous

Two Marks

Untamed

Tempted

Desired

Enticed

More Than A Cowboy

Strong & Steady

Rough & Ready

Wild Mountain Men

Mountain Darkness

Mountain Delights

Mountain Desire

Mountain Danger

Grade-A Beefcakes

Sir Loin of Beef

T-Bone

Tri-Tip

Porterhouse

Skirt Steak

Big Sky Boyfriends

Misadventures of a Single Mom

Misadventures with the Mistaken Twin

Misadventures with my Billionaire Boss

Misadventures with my Fake Fiancé

Misadventures and Ms. Demeanor

Steele Ranch

Spurred

Wrangled

Tangled

Hitched

Lassoed

Bridgewater County

Ride Me Dirty

Claim Me Hard

Take Me Fast

Hold Me Close

Make Me Yours

Kiss Me Crazy

Mail Order Bride of Slate Springs

A Wanton Woman

A Wild Woman

A Wicked Woman

Bridgewater Brides

Their Runaway Bride

Their Kidnapped Bride

Their Wayward Bride

Their Captivated Bride

Their Treasured Bride

Their Christmas Bride

Their Reluctant Bride

Their Stolen Bride

Their Brazen Bride

Their Rebellious Bride

Their Reckless Bride

Lenox Ranch Cowboys

Cowboys & Kisses

Spurs & Satin

Reins & Ribbons

Brands & Bows

Lassos & Lace

Montana Men

The Lawman

The Cowboy

The Outlaw

The Billion Heirs

Scarred

Flawed

Broken

Standalones

Relentless

Bride Pact

Rough Love

Twice As Delicious

Flirting With The Law

Mistletoe Marriage

Man Candy - A Coloring Book

ABOUT RENEE ROSE

USA TODAY BESTSELLING AUTHOR RENEE ROSE loves a dominant, dirty-talking alpha hero! Readers have devoured over five million copies of her steamy romance with varying levels of kink. Her books have been featured in USA Today's *Happily Ever After* and *Popsugar*. Named Eroticon USA's Next Top Erotic Author in 2013, she has also won *Spunky and Sassy's* Favorite Sci-Fi and Anthology author, *The Romance Reviews* Best Historical Romance, and has hit the *USA Today* list fifteen times with her Bad Boy Alphas, Chicago Bratva, and Wolf Ranch series.

Renee loves to connect with readers!
www.reneeroseromance.com
reneeroseauthor@gmail.com

facebook.com/reneeroseromance
instagram.com/reneeroseromance
bookbub.com/authors/renee-rose
tiktok.com/@reneeroseromance

ABOUT VANESSA VALE

A USA Today bestseller, Vanessa Vale writes tempting romance with unapologetic bad boys who don't just fall in love, they fall hard. Her books have sold over one million copies. She lives in the American West where she's always finding inspiration for her next story.

vanessavaleauthor.com

facebook.com/vanessavaleauthor

instagram.com/vanessa_vale_author

amazon.com/author/vanessavale

bookbub.com/profile/vanessa-vale

tiktok.com/@vanessavaleauthor